D0532247

Success Stories

RUSSELL BANKS

HARPER & ROW, PUBLISHERS, New York
Cambridge, Philadelphia, San Francisco, London
Mexico City, São Paulo, Singapore, Sydney

1817

Some of the stories in this collection originally appeared in *The Agni Review, Chicago, Esquire, Fiction, Mother Jones, Pequod, Sun & Moon: A Journal of Literature & Art,* and *Vanity Fair.*

"Sarah Cole: A Type of Love Story" originally appeared in *The Missouri Review.* It was included in *The Best American Short Stories 1985* and *The Pushcart Prize: Anthology 1985.*

FIRST EDITION

Designer: Sidney Feinberg

Library of Congress Cataloging-in-Publication Data

Banks, Russell, 1940—
    Success stories.

    I. Title.
PS3552.A49S8   1986   813.'54   85-45617
ISBN 0-06-015567-1

---

86 87 88 89 90 RRD 10 9 8 7 6 5 4 3 2 1

for Linda and Steve

Contents

Queen
for a
Day

The elder of the two boys, Earl, turns from the dimly lit worktable, a door on sawhorses, where he is writing. He pauses a second and says to his brother, "Cut that out, willya? Getcha feet off the walls."

The other boy says, "Don't tell me what to do. You're not the boss of this family, you know." He is dark-haired with large brown eyes, a moody ten-year-old lying bored on his cot with sneakered feet slapped against the faded green floral print wallpaper.

Earl crosses his arms over his bony chest and stares down at his brother from a considerable height. The room is cluttered with model airplanes, schoolbooks, papers, clothing, hockey sticks and skates, a set of barbells. Earl says, "We're supposed to be doing homework, you know. If she hears you tramping your feet on the walls, she'll come in here screaming. So get your damned feet off the wall. I ain't kidding."

"She can't hear me. Besides, you ain't doing homework. And *I'm* reading," he says, waving a geography book at him.

The older boy sucks his breath through his front teeth and glares. "You really piss me off, George. Just put your goddamned feet down, will you? I can't concentrate with you doing that, rubbing your feet all over the wallpaper like you're doing. It makes me all distracted." He turns back to his writing, scribbling with a ballpoint pen on lined paper in a schoolboy's three-ring binder. Earl has sandy blond hair and pale blue eyes that turn downward at the corners and a full red mouth. He's more scrawny than skinny, hard and flat-muscled, and suddenly tall for his age, making him a head taller than his brother, taller even than their mother now, too, and able to pat their sister's head as if he were a full-grown adult already.

He turned twelve eight months ago, in March, and in May their father left. Their father is a union carpenter who works on projects in distant corners of the state—schools, hospitals, post offices—and for a whole year the man came home only on weekends. Then, for a while, every other weekend. Finally, he was gone for a month, and when he came home the last time, it was to say goodbye to Earl, George, and their sister Louise, and to their mother, too, of course, she who had been saying (for what seemed to the children years) that she never wanted to see the man again anyhow, ever, under any circumstances, because he just causes trouble when he's home and more trouble when he doesn't come home, so he might as well stay away for good. They can all get along better without him, she insisted, which was true, Earl was sure, but that was before the man left for good and stopped sending them money, so that now, six months later, Earl is not so sure anymore that they can get along better without their father than with him.

It happened on a Sunday morning, a day washed with new sunshine and dry air, with the whole family standing somberly in the kitchen, summoned there from their rooms by their mother's taut, high-pitched voice, a voice that had an awful point to prove. "Come out here! Your father has something important to say to you!"

They obeyed, one by one, and gathered in a line before their father, who, dressed in pressed khakis and shined work shoes and cap, sat at the kitchen table, a pair of suitcases beside him, and in front of him a cup of coffee, which he stirred slowly with a spoon. His eyes were red and filled with dense water, the way they almost always were on Sunday mornings, from his drinking the night before, the children knew, and he had trouble looking them in the face, because of the sorts of things he and their mother were heard saying to one another when they were at home together late Saturday nights. On this Sunday morning it was only a little worse than usual—his hands shook some, and he could barely hold his cigarette; he let it smolder in the ashtray and kept on stirring his coffee while he talked. "Your mother and me," he said in his low, roughened voice, "we've decided on some things you kids should know about." He cleared his throat. "Your mother, she thinks you oughta hear it from me, though I don't quite know so much about that as she does, since it isn't completely my idea alone." He studied his coffee cup for a few seconds.

"They should hear it from you because it's what you *want!*" their mother finally said. She stood by the sink, her hands wringing each other dry, and stared over at the man. Her face was swollen and red from crying, which, for the children, was not an unusual thing to see on a Sunday morning when their father was home. They still did not know what was coming.   •

"Adele, it's *not* what I want," he said. "It's what's got to be, that's all. Kids," he said, "I got to leave you folks for a while. A long while. And I won't be comin' back, I guess." He grabbed his cigarette with thumb and forefinger and inhaled the smoke fiercely, then placed the butt back into the ashtray and went on talking, as if to the table: "I don't want to do this, I hate it, but I got to. It's too hard to explain, and I'm hoping that someday you'll understand it all, but I just . . . I just got to live somewheres else now."

Louise, the little girl, barely six years old, was the only one of the three children who could speak. She said, "Where are you going, Daddy?"

"Upstate," he said. "Back up to Holderness, where I been

all along. I got me an apartment up there, small place."

"That's not all he's got up there!" their mother said.

"Adele, I can walk outa here right this second," he said smoothly. "I don't hafta explain a damned thing, if you keep that kinda stuff up. We had an agreement."

"Yup, yup. Sorry," she said, pursing her lips, locking them with an invisible key, throwing the key away.

Finally, Earl could speak. "Will . . . will you come and see us, or can we come visit you, on weekends and like that?" he asked his father.

"Sure, son, you can visit me, anytime you want. It'll take a while for me to get the place set up right, but soon's I get it all set up for kids, I'll call you, and we'll work out some nice visits. I shouldn't come here, though, not for a while. You understand."

Earl shook his head somberly up and down, as if his one anxiety concerning this event had been put satisfactorily to rest.

George had turned his back on his father, however, and now he was taking tiny, mincing half-steps across the linoleum-covered kitchen floor toward the outside door. Then he stopped a second, opened the door and stood on the landing at the top of the stairs, and no one tried to stop him, because he was doing what they wanted to do themselves, and then they heard him running pell-mell, as if falling, down the darkened stairs, two flights, to the front door of the building, heard it slam behind him, and knew he was gone, up Perley Street, between parked cars, down alleys, to a hiding place where they knew he'd stop, sit, and bawl, knew it because it was what they wanted to do themselves, especially Earl, who was too old, too scared, too confused and too angry. Instead of running away and bawling, Earl said, "I hope everyone can be more happy now."

His father smiled and looked at him for the first time and clapped him on the shoulder. "Hey, son," he said, "you, you're the man of the house now. I know you can do it.

You're a good kid, and listen, I'm proud of you. Your mother, your brother and sister, they're all going to need you a hell of a lot more than they have before, but I know you're up to it, son. I'm countin' on ya," he said, and he stood up and rubbed out his cigarette. Then he reached beyond Earl with both hands and hugged Earl's little sister, lifted her off her feet and squeezed her tight, and when the man set her down, he wiped tears away from his eyes. "Tell Georgie . . . well, maybe I'll see him downstairs or something. He's upset, I guess. . . ." He shook Earl's hand, drew him close, quickly hugged him and let go and stepped away. Grabbing up his suitcases, in silence, without looking over once at his wife or back at his children, he left the apartment.

For good. "And good riddance, too," as their mother immediately started saying to anyone who would listen. Louise said she missed her daddy, but she seemed to be quickly forgetting that, since for most of her life he had worked away from home, and George, who stayed mad, went deep inside himself and said nothing about it at all, and Earl—who did not know how he felt about their father's abandoning them, for he knew that in many ways it was the best their father could do for them and in many other ways it was the worst— spoke of the man as if he had died in an accident, as if their mother were a widow and they half orphaned. This freed him, though he did not know it then, to concentrate on survival, survival for them all, which he now understood to be his personal responsibility, for his mother seemed utterly incapable of guaranteeing it and his brother and sister, of course, were still practically babies. Often, late at night, lying in his squeaky, narrow cot next to his brother's, Earl would say to himself, "I'm the man of the house now," and somehow just saying it, over and over, "I'm the man of the house now," like a prayer, made his terror ease back away from his face, and he could finally slip into sleep.

Now, with his father gone six months and their mother still fragile, still denouncing the man to everyone who listens, and even to those who don't listen but merely show her their faces for a moment or two, it's as if the man were still coming home weekends drunk and raging against her and the world, were still betraying her, were telling all her secrets to another woman in a motel room in the northern part of the state. It's as if he were daily abandoning her and their three children over and over again, agreeing to send money and then sending nothing, promising to call and write letters and then going silent on them, planning visits and trips together on weekends and holidays and then leaving them with not even a forwarding address, forbidding them, almost, from adjusting to a new life, a life in which their father and her husband does not betray them anymore.

Earl decides to solve their problems himself. He hatches and implements, as best he can, plans, schemes, designs, all intended to find a substitute for the lost father. He introduces his mother to his hockey coach, who turns out to be married and a new father; and he invites in for breakfast and to meet his ma the cigar-smoking vet with the metal plate in his skull who drops off the newspapers at dawn for Earl to deliver before school, but the man turns out to dislike women actively enough to tell Earl so, right to his face: "No offense, kid, I'm sure your ma's a nice lady, but I got no use for 'em is why I'm single, not 'cause I ain't met the right one yet or something"; and to the guy who comes to read the electric meter one afternoon when Earl's home from school with the flu and his mother's at work down at the tannery, where they've taken her on as an assistant bookkeeper, Earl says that he can't let the man into the basement because it's locked and he'll have to come back later when his mom's home, so she can let him in herself, and the man says, "Hey, no problem, I can use last month's reading and make the correction next month," and waves cheerfully goodbye, leaving Earl suddenly, utterly, shockingly aware of his foolishness, his pathetic, helpless longing for a man of the house.

For a moment, he blames his mother for his longing and

hates her for his fantasies. But then quickly he forgives her and blames himself and commences to concoct what he thinks of as more realistic, more dignified plans, schemes, designs: sweepstakes tickets, lotteries, raffles—Earl buys tickets on the sly with his paper route money. And he enters contests, essay contests for junior high school students that provide the winner with a week-long trip for him and a parent to Washington, D.C., and the National Spelling Bee, which takes Earl only to the county level before he fails to spell "alligator" correctly. A prize, any kind of award from the world outside their tiny, besieged family, Earl believes, will make their mother happy at last. He believes that a prize will validate their new life somehow and will thus separate it, once and for all, from their father. It will be as if their father never existed.

"So what are you writing now?" George demands from the bed. He walks his feet up the wall as high as he can reach, then retreats. "I know it ain't homework, you don't write that fast when you're doing homework. What is it, a *love* letter?" He leers.

"No, asshole. Just take your damned feet off the wall, will you? Ma's gonna be in here in a minute screaming at both of us." Earl closes the notebook and pushes it away from him carefully, as if it is the Bible and he has just finished reading aloud from it.

"I wanna see what you wrote," George says, flipping around and setting his feet, at last, onto the floor. He reaches toward the notebook. "Lemme see it."

"C'mon, willya? Cut the shit."

"Naw, lemme see it." He stands up and swipes the notebook from the table as Earl moves to protect it.

"You little sonofabitch!" Earl says, and he clamps onto the notebook with both hands and yanks, pulling George off his feet and forward onto Earl's lap, and they both tumble to the floor, where they begin to fight, swing fists and knees, roll and grab, bumping against furniture in the tiny, crowded room, until a lamp falls over, books tumble to the floor, model airplanes crash. In seconds, George is getting the worst of it and scrambles across the floor to the door, with Earl crawling along behind, yanking his brother's shirt with one hand and pounding at his head and back with the other, when suddenly the bedroom door swings open, and their mother stands over them. Grabbing both boys by their collars, she shrieks, "What's the matter with you! What're you doing! What're you doing!" They stop and collapse into a bundle of legs and arms, but she goes on shrieking at them. "I can't *stand* it when you fight! Don't you know that? I can't *stand* it!"

George cries, "I didn't do anything! I just wanted to see his homework!"

"Yeah, sure," Earl says. "Sure. Innocent as a baby."

"Shut up! Both of you!" their mother screams. She is wild-eyed, glaring down at them, and, as he has done so many times, Earl looks at her face as if he's outside his body, and he sees that she's not angry at them at all, she's frightened and in pain, as if her sons are little animals, rats or ferrets, with tiny, razor-sharp teeth biting at her ankles and feet.

Quickly, Earl gets to his feet and says, "I'm sorry, Ma. I guess I'm just a little tired or something lately." He pats his mother on her shoulder and offers a small smile. George crawls on hands and knees back to his bed and lies on it, while Earl gently turns their mother around and steers her back out the door to the living room, where the television set drones on, Les Paul and Mary Ford, playing their guitars and singing bland harmonies. "We'll be out in a few minutes for *Dobie Gillis*, Ma. Don't worry," Earl says.

"Jeez," George says. "How can she stand that Les Paul and Mary Ford stuff? Yuck. Even Louise goes to bed when it comes on, and it's only what, six-thirty?"

"Yeah. Shut up."

"Up yours."

Earl leans down and scoops up the fallen dictionary, pens, airplanes and lamp and places them back on the worktable.

The black binder he opens squarely in front of him, and he says to his brother, "Here, you wanta see what I was writing? Go ahead and read it. I don't care."

"I don't care, either. Unless it's a *love* letter!"

"No, it's not a *love* letter."

"What is it, then?"

"Nothing," Earl says, closing the notebook. "Homework."

"Oh," George says, and he starts marching his feet up the wall and back again.

Nov. 7, 1953

Dear Jack Bailey,

    I think my mother should be queen for a day because she has suffered a lot more than most mothers in this life and she has come out of it very cheerful and loving. The most important fact is that my father left her alone with three children, myself (age 12½), my brother George (age 10), and my sister Louise (age 6). He left her for another woman though that's not the important thing, because my mother has risen above all that. But he refuses to send her any child support money. He's been gone over six months and we still haven't seen one cent. My mother went to a lawyer but the lawyer wants $50 in advance to help her take my father to court. She has a job as assistant bookkeeper down at Belvedere's Tannery downtown and the pay is bad, barely enough for our rent and food costs in fact, so where is she going to get $50 for a lawyer?

    Also my father was a very cruel man who drinks too much and many times when he was living with us when he came home from work he was drunk and he would beat her. This has caused her and us kids a lot of nervous suffering and now she sometimes has spells which the doctor says are serious, though he doesn't know exactly what they are.

    We used to have a car and my father left it with us

when he left (a big favor) because he had a pickup truck. But he owed over $450 on the car to the bank so the bank came and repossessed the car. Now my mother has to walk everywhere she goes which is hard and causes her varicose veins and takes a lot of valuable time from her day.

My sister Louise needs glasses the school nurse said but "Who can pay for them?" my mother says. My paper route gets a little money but it's barely enough for school lunches for the three of us kids which is what we use it for.

My mother's two sisters and her brother haven't been too helpful because they are Catholic, as she is and the rest of us, and they don't believe in divorce and think that she should not have let my father leave her anyhow. She needs to get a divorce but no one except me and my brother George think it is a good idea. Therefore my mother cries a lot at night because she feels so abandoned in this time of her greatest need.

The rest of the time though she is cheerful and loving in spite of her troubles and nervousness. That is why I believe that this courageous long-suffering woman, my mother, should be Queen for a Day.

Sincerely yours,
Earl Painter

Several weeks slide by, November gets cold and gray, and a New Hampshire winter starts to feel inevitable again, and Earl does not receive the letter he expects. He has told no one, especially his mother, that he has written to Jack Bailey, the smiling, mustachioed host of the *Queen for a Day* television show, which Earl happened to see that time he was home for several days with the flu, bored and watching television all afternoon. Afterwards, delivering papers in the predawn gloom, in school all day, at the hockey rink, doing homework at night, he could not forget about the television show, the sad stories told by the contestants about their illness, poverty, neglect, victimization and, always, their bad luck, luck so bad that you feel it's somehow deserved. The studio audience seemed genuinely saddened, moved to tears, even, by Jack Bailey's recitation of these narratives, and then elated afterwards, when the winning victims, all of them middle-aged women, were rewarded with refrigerators, living room suites, vacation trips, washing machines, china, fur coats and, if they needed them, wheelchairs, prosthetic limbs, twenty-four-hour nursing care. As these women wept for joy, the audience applauded, and Earl almost applauded too, alone there in the dim living room of the small, cold, and threadbare apartment in a mill town in central New Hampshire.

Earl knows that those women's lives surely aren't much different from his mother's life, and in fact, if he has told it right, if somehow he has got into the letter what he has intuited is basically wrong with his mother's life, it will be obvious to everyone in the audience that his mother's life is actually much worse than that of many or perhaps even most of the women who win the prizes. Earl knows that though his mother enjoys good health (except for "spells") and holds down a job and is able to feed, house, and clothe her children, there is still a deep, essential sadness in her life that, in his eyes, none of the contestants on *Queen for a Day* has. He believes that if he can just get his description of her life right, other people—Jack Bailey, the studio audience, millions of people all over America watching it on television —*everyone* will share in her sadness, so that when she is rewarded with appliances, furniture and clothing, maybe even a trip to Las Vegas, then everyone will share in her elation, too. Even he will share in it.

Earl knows that it is not easy to become a contestant on *Queen for a Day*. Somehow your letter describing the candidate has first to move Jack Bailey, and then your candidate has to be able to communicate her sufferings over television in a clear and dramatic way. Earl noticed that some of the contestants, to their own apparent disadvantage, downplayed the effect on them of certain tragedies—a child with a birth defect, say, or an embarrassing kind of operation or a humiliating dismissal by an employer—while playing up other, seemingly less disastrous events, such as being cheated out of a small inheritance by a phony siding contractor or having to drop out of hairdressing school because of a parent's illness, and when the studio audience was asked to show the extent and depth of its compassion by having its applause measured on a meter, it was always the woman who managed to present the most convincing mixture of courage and complaint who won.

Earl supposes that what happens is that Jack Bailey writes or maybe telephones the writer of the letter nominating a particular woman for *Queen for a Day* and offers him and his nominee the opportunity to come to New York City's Radio City Music Hall to tell her story in person, and then, based on how she does in the audition, Jack Bailey chooses her and two other nominees for a particular show, maybe next week, when they all come back to New York City to tell their stories live on television. Thus, daily, when Earl arrives home, he asks Louise and George, who normally get home from school an hour or so earlier than he, if there's any mail for him, any letter. You're sure? Nothing? No phone calls, either?

"Who're you expectin' to hear from, lover boy, your *girl* friend?" George grins, teeth spotted with peanut butter and gobs of white bread.

"Up yours," Earl says, and heads into his bedroom, where he dumps his coat, books, hockey gear. It's becoming clear to him that if there's such a thing as a success, he's evidently a failure. If there's such a thing as a winner, he's a loser. I oughta go on that goddamned show myself, he thinks. Flopping onto his bed face-first, he wishes he could keep on falling, as if down a bottomless well or mine shaft, into darkness and warmth, lost and finally blameless, gone, gone, gone. And soon he is asleep, dreaming of a hockey game, and he's carrying the puck, dragging it all the way up along the right, digging in close to the boards, skate blades flashing as he cuts around behind the net, ice chips spraying in white fantails, and when he comes out on the other side, he looks down in front of him and can't find the puck, it's gone, dropped off behind him, lost in his sweeping turn, the spray, the slash of the skates and the long sweeping arc of the stick in front of him. He brakes, turns, and heads back, searching for the small black disk.

At the sound of the front door closing, a quiet click, as if someone is deliberately trying to enter the apartment silently, Earl wakes from his dream, and he hears voices from the kitchen, George and Louise and his mother:

"Hi, Mom. We're just makin' a snack, peanut butter sandwiches."

"Mommy, George won't give me—"

"Don't eat it directly off the knife like that!"

"Sorry, I was jus'—"

"You heard me, mister, don't answer back!"

"Jeez, I was jus'—"

"I don't *care* what you were doing!" Her voice is trembling and quickly rising in pitch and timbre, and Earl moves off his bed and comes into the kitchen, smiling, drawing everyone's attention to him, the largest person in the room, the only one with a smile on his face, a relaxed, easy, sociable face and manner, normalcy itself, as he gives his brother's shoulder a fraternal squeeze, tousles his sister's brown hair, nods hello to his mother and says, "Hey, you're home early, Ma. What happened, they give you guys the rest of the day off?"

Then he sees her face, white, tight, drawn back in a cadaverous grimace, her pale blue eyes wild, unfocused, rolling back, and he says, "Jeez, Ma, what's the matter, you okay?"

Her face breaks into pieces, goes from dry to wet, white to red, and she is weeping loudly, blubbering, wringing her hands in front of her like a maddened knitter. "Aw-w-w-w!" she wails, and Louise and George, too, start to cry. They run to her and wrap her in their arms, crying and begging her not to cry, as Earl, aghast, sits back in his chair and watches the three of them wind around each other like snakes moving in and out of one another's coils.

"Stop!" he screams at last. "Stop it! All of you!" He pounds his fists on the table. "Stop crying, all of you!"

And they obey him, George first, then their mother, then Louise, who goes on staring into her mother's face. George looks at his feet, ashamed, and their mother looks pleadingly into Earl's face, expectant, hopeful, as if knowing that he will organize everything.

In a calm voice, Earl says, "Ma, tell me what happened. Just say it slowly, you know, and it'll come out okay, and then we can all talk about it, okay?"

She nods, and slowly George unravels his arms from around her neck and steps away from her, moving to the far wall of the room, where he stands and looks out the window and down to the bare yard below. Louise snuggles her face in close to her mother and sniffles quietly.

"I . . . I lost my job. I got fired today," their mother says. "And it wasn't my fault," she says, starting to weep again, and Louise joins her, bawling now, and George at the window starts to sob, his small shoulders heaving.

Earl shouts, "Wait! Wait a minute, Ma, just *tell* me about it. Don't cry!" he commands her, and she shudders, draws herself together again and continues.

"I . . . I had some problems this morning, a bunch of files I was supposed to put away last week sometime got lost. And everybody was running around like crazy looking for them, 'cause they had all these figures from last year's sales in 'em or something, I don't know. Anyhow, they were important, and I was the one who was accused of losing them. Which

I didn't! But no one could find them, until finally they turned
up on Robbie's desk, down in shipping, which I couldna done
since I never go to shipping anyhow. But just the same, Rose
blamed me, because she's the head bookkeeper and she was
the last person to use the files, and she was getting it because
they needed them upstairs, and . . . well, you know, I was
just getting yelled at and yelled at, and it went on after lunch
. . . and, I don't know, I just started feeling dizzy and all, you
know, like I was going to black out again? And I guess I got
scared and started talking real fast, so Rose took me down
to the nurse, and I did black out then. Only for a few seconds,
though, and when I felt a little better, Rose said maybe I
should go home for the rest of the day, which is what I
wanted to do anyhow. But when I went back upstairs to get
my pocketbook and coat and my lunch, because I hadn't
been able to eat my sandwich, even, I was so nervous and
all, and then Mr. Shandy called me into his office. . . ." She
makes a twisted little smile, helpless and confused, and
quickly continues. "Mr. Shandy said I should maybe take a
lot of time off. Two weeks sick leave with pay, he said, even
though I was only working there six months. He said that
would give me time to look for another job, one that
wouldn't cause me so much worry, he said. So I said, 'Are
you firing me?' and he said, 'Yes, I am,' just like that. 'But
it would be better for you all around,' he said, 'if you left for
medical reasons or something.' "

Earl slowly exhales. He's been holding his breath
throughout, though from her very first sentence he has
known what the outcome would be. Reaching forward, he
takes his mother's hands in his, stroking them as if they were
an injured bird. He doesn't know what will happen now, but
somehow he is not afraid. Not really. Yet he knows that he
should be terrified, and when he says this to himself, *I should
be terrified,* he answers by observing simply that this is not
the worst thing. The worst thing that can happen to them
is that one or all of them will die. And because he is still a

child, or at least enough of a child not to believe in death, he knows that no one in his family is going to die. He cannot share this secret comfort with anyone in the family, however. His brother and sister, children completely, cannot yet know that death is the worst thing that can happen to them; they think this is, that their mother has been fired from her job, which is why they are crying. And his mother, no longer a child at all, cannot believe with Earl that the worst thing will not happen, for this is too much like death and may somehow lead directly to it, which is why she is crying. Only Earl can refuse to cry. Which he does.

Later, in the room she shares with her daughter, their mother lies fully clothed on the double bed and sleeps, and it grows dark, and while George and Louise watch television in the gloom of the living room, Earl writes:

Nov. 21, 1953

Dear Jack Bailey,

Maybe my first letter to you about why my mother should be queen for a day did not reach you or else I just didn't write it good enough for you to want her on your show. But I thought I would write again anyhow, if that's okay, and mention to you a few things that I left out of that first letter and also mention again some of the things in that letter, in case you did not get it at all for some reason (you know the Post Office). I also want to mention a few new developments that have made things even worse for my poor mother than they already were.

First, even though it's only a few days until Thanksgiving my father who left us last May, as you know, has not contacted us about the holidays or offered to help in any way. This makes us mad though we don't talk about it much since the little kids tend to cry about it a lot when they think about it, and me and my mother think it's best not to think about it. We don't even know

how to write a letter to my father, though we know the
name of the company that he works for up in Holderness
(a town in New Hampshire pretty far from here) and his
sisters could tell us his address if we asked, but we won't.
A person has to have some pride, as my mother says.
Which she has a lot of.

We will get through Thanksgiving all right because
of St. Joseph's Church, which is where we go sometimes
and where I was confirmed and my brother George (age
10) took his first communion last year and where my sister Louise (age 6) goes to catechism class. St. Joe's (as we
call it) has turkeys and other kinds of food for people who
can't afford to buy one so we'll do okay if my mother
goes down there and says she can't afford to buy a turkey
for her family on Thanksgiving. This brings me to the
new developments.

My mother just got fired from her job as assistant
bookkeeper at the tannery. It wasn't her fault or anything she did. They just fired her because she has these
nervous spells sometimes when there's a lot of pressure
on her, which is something that happens a lot these days
because of my father and all and us kids and the rest of
it. She got two weeks of pay but that's the only money
we have until she gets another job. Tomorrow she plans
to go downtown to all the stores and try to get a job as a
saleslady now that Christmas is coming and the stores
hire a lot of extras. But right now we don't have any
money for anything like Thanksgiving turkey or pies, and
we can't go down to Massachusetts to my mother's family, Aunt Dot's and Aunt Leona's and Uncle Jerry's house,
like we used to because (as you know) the bank repos-
sessed the car. And my father's sisters and all who used
to have Thanksgiving with us, sometimes, have taken our
father's side in this because of his lies about us and now
they won't talk to us anymore.

I know that lots and lots of people are poor as us

and many of them are sick too, or crippled from polio
and other bad diseases. But I still think my mother
should be Queen for a Day because of other things.

Because even though she's poor and got fired and
has dizzy spells and sometimes blacks out, she's a proud
woman. And even though my father walked off and left
all his responsibilities behind, she stayed here with us.
And in spite of all her troubles and worries, she really
does take good care of his children. One look in her eyes
and you know it.

Thank you very much for listening to me and con-
sidering my mother for the Queen for a Day television
show.

Sincerely,
Earl Painter

The day before Thanksgiving their mother is hired to
start work the day after Thanksgiving, in gift wrapping at
Grover Cronin's on Moody Street, and consequently she
does not feel ashamed for accepting a turkey and a bag of
groceries from St. Joe's. "Since I'm working, I don't think of
it as charity. I think of it as a kind of loan," she explains to
Earl as they walk the four blocks to the church.

It's dark, though still late afternoon, and cold, almost cold
enough to snow, Earl thinks, which makes him think of
Christmas, which in turn makes him cringe and tremble inside and turn quickly back to now, to this very moment, to
walking with his tiny, brittle-bodied mother down the quiet
street, past houses like their own—triple-decker wood-frame
tenements, each with a wide front porch like a bosom facing
the narrow street below, lights on in kitchens in back, where
mothers make boiled supper for kids cross-legged on the living room floor watching *Kukla, Fran and Ollie,* while dads
trudge up from the mills by the river or drive in from one
of the plants on the Heights or maybe walk home from one
of the stores downtown, the A&P, J. C. Penney's, Sears—the

homes of ordinary families, people exactly like them. But with one crucial difference, for a piece is missing from the Painter family, a keystone, making all other families, in Earl's eyes, wholly different from his, and for an anxious moment he envies them. He wants to turn up a walkway to a strange house, step up to the door, open it and walk down the long, dark, sweet-smelling hallway to the kitchen in back, say hi and toss his coat over a chair and sit down for supper, have his father growl at him to hang his coat up and wash his hands first, have his mother ask about school today, how did hockey practice go, have his sister interrupt to show her broken dolly to their father, beg him to fix it, which he does at the table next to his son, waiting for supper to be put on the table, all of them relaxed, happy, relieved that tomorrow is a holiday, a day at home with the family, no work, no school, no hockey practice. Tomorrow, he and his father and his brother will go to the high school football game at noon and will be home by two to help set the table.

Earl's mother says, "That job down at Grover Cronin's? It's only, it's a temporary job, you know." She says it as if uttering a slightly shameful secret. "After Christmas I get let go."

Earl jams his hands deeper into his jacket pockets and draws his chin down inside his collar. "Yeah, I figured."

"And the money, well, the money's not much. It's almost nothing. I added it up, for a week and for a month, and it comes out to quite a lot less than what you and me figured out in that budget, for the rent and food and all. What we need. It's less than what we need. Never mind Christmas, even. Just regular."

They stop a second at a curb, wait for a car to pass, then cross the street and turn right. Elm trees loom in black columns overhead; leafless branches spread out in high arcs and cast intricate shadows on the sidewalk below. Earl can hear footsteps click against the pavement, his own off-beat, long stride and her short, quick one combining in a stuttered rhythm. He says, "You gotta take the job, though, doncha? I mean, there isn't anything else, is there? Not now, anyhow. Maybe soon, though, Ma, in a few days, maybe, if something at the store opens up in one of the other departments, dresses or something. Bookkeeping, maybe. You never know, Ma."

"No, you're right. Things surprise you. Still . . ." She sighs, pushing a cloud of breath out in front of her. "But I am glad for the turkey and the groceries. We'll have a nice Thanksgiving, anyhow," she chirps.

"Yeah."

They are silent for a few seconds, still walking, and then she says, "I been talking to Father LaCoy, Earl. You know, about . . . about our problems. I been asking his advice. He's a nice man, not just a priest, you know, but a kind man too. He knows your father, he knew him years and years ago, when they were in high school together. He said he was a terrible drinker even then. And he said . . . other things, he said some things the other morning that I been thinking about."

"What morning?"

"Day before yesterday. Early. When you were doing your papers. I felt I just had to talk to someone, I was all nervous and worried, and I needed to talk to someone here at St. Joe's anyhow, 'cause I wanted to know about how to get the turkey and all, so I came over, and he was saying the early mass, so I stayed and talked with him a while afterwards. He's a nice priest, I like him. I always liked Father LaCoy."

"Yeah. What'd he say?" Earl knows already what the priest said, and he pulls himself further down inside his jacket, where his insides seem to have hardened like an ingot, cold and dense, at the exact center of his body.

Up ahead, at the end of the block, is St. Joseph's, a large, squat parish church with a short, broad steeple, built late in the last century of pale yellow stone cut from a quarry up on the Heights and hauled across the river in winter on sledges. "Father LaCoy says that your father and me, we should try to get back together. That we should start over, so to speak."

"And you think he's right," Earl adds.

"Well, not exactly. Not just like that. I mean, he knows what happened. He knows all about your father and all, I told him, but he knew anyhow. I told him how it was, but he told me that it's not right for us to be going on like this, without a father and all. So he said, he told me, he'd like to arrange to have a meeting in his office at the church, a meeting between me and your father, so we could maybe talk some of our problems out. And make some compromises, he said."

Earl is nearly a full head taller than his mother, but suddenly, for the first time since before his father left, he feels small, a child again, helpless, dependent, pulled this mysterious way or that by the obscure needs and desires of adults. "Yeah, but how come . . . how come Father LaCoy thinks Daddy'll even listen? He doesn't *want* us!"

"I know, I know," his mother murmurs. "But what can I do? What else can I do?"

Earl has stopped walking and shouts at his mother, like a dog barking at the end of a leash: "He can't even get in touch with Daddy! He doesn't even know where Daddy is!"

She stops and speaks in a steady voice. "Yes, he can find him all right. I told him where Daddy was working and gave him the name of McGrath and Company and also Aunt Ellie's number too. So he can get in touch with him, if he wants to. He's a priest."

"A priest can get in touch with him but his own wife and kids can't!"

His mother has pulled up now and looks at her son with a hardness in her face that he can't remember having seen before. She tells him, "You don't understand. I know how hard it's been for you, Earl, all this year, from way back, even, with all the fighting, and then when your father went away. But you got to understand a little bit how it's been for me, too. I can't . . . I can't do this all alone like this."

"Do you love Daddy?" he demands. *"Do* you? After . . . after everything he's done? After hitting you like he did all those times, and the yelling and all, and the drinking, and then, then the worst, after leaving us like he did! Leaving us and running off with that *girl*friend or whatever of his! And not sending any money! Making you hafta go to work, with us kids coming home after school and nobody at home. Ma, he *left* us! Don't you know that? He *left* us!" Earl is weeping now. His skinny arms wrapped around his own chest, tears streaming over his cheeks, the boy stands straight-legged and stiff on the sidewalk in the golden glow of the streetlight, his wet face crossed with spidery shadows from the elm trees, and he shouts, "I *hate* him! I hate him, and I never want him to come back again! If you let him come back, I swear it, I'm gonna run away! I'll leave!"

His mother says, "Oh, no, Earl, you don't mean that," and she reaches forward to hold him, but he backs fiercely away.

"No! I do mean it! If you let him back into our house, I'm leaving."

"Earl. Where will you go? You're just a boy."

"Ma, so help me, don't treat me like this. I can go lotsa places, don't worry. I can go to Boston, I can go to Florida, I can go to lotsa places. All I got to do is hitchhike. I'm not a little kid anymore," he says, and he draws himself up and looks down at her.

"You *don't* hate your father."

"Yes, Ma. Yes, I do. And you should hate him too. After all he did to you."

They are silent for a moment, facing each other, looking into each other's pale blue eyes. He is her son, his face is her face, not his father's. Earl and his mother have the same sad, downward-turning eyes, like teardrops, the same full red mouth, the same clear voice, and now, at this moment, they share the same agony, a life-bleeding pain that can be stanched only with a lie, a denial.

She says, "All right, then. I'll tell Father LaCoy. I'll tell him that I don't want to talk to your father, it's gone too far now. I'll tell him that I'm going to get a divorce." She opens her arms, and her son steps into them. Above her head, his eyes jammed shut, he holds on to his tiny mother and sobs, as if he's learned that his father has died.

His mother says, "I don't know when I'll get the divorce, Earl, but I'll do it. Things'll work out. They have to. Right?" she asks, as if asking a baby who can't understand her words.

He nods. "Yeah . . . yeah, things'll work out," he says.

They let go of one another and walk slowly on toward the church.

                                                    Dec. 12, 1953

Dear Jack Bailey,

Yes, it's me again and this is my third letter asking you to make my mother Adele Painter into queen for a day. Things are much worse now than last time I wrote to you. I had to quit the hockey team so I could take an extra paper route in the afternoons because my mother's job at Grover Cronin's is minimum wage and can't pay our bills. But that's okay, it's only junior high so it doesn't matter like if I was in high school as I will be next year. So I don't really mind.

My mother hasn't had any of her spells lately, but she's still really nervous and cries a lot and yells a lot at the kids over little things because she's so worried about money and everything. We had to get winter coats and boots this year used from the church, St. Joe's, and my mom cried a lot about that. Now that Christmas is so close everything reminds her of how poor we are now, even her job which is wrapping gifts. She has to stand on her feet six days and three nights a week so her varicose veins are a lot worse than before, so when she comes home she usually has to go right to bed.

My brother George comes home now after school and takes care of Louise until I get through delivering

papers and can come home and make supper for us, because my mother's usually at work then. We don't feel
too sad because we've got each other and we all love
each other but it is hard to feel happy a lot of the time,
especially at Christmas.

My mother paid out over half of one week's pay as
a down payment to get a lawyer to help her get a divorce from my father and get the court to make him pay
her some child support, but the lawyer said it might take
two months for any money to come and the divorce can't
be done until next June. The lawyer also wrote a letter to
my father to try and scare him into paying us some
money but so far it hasn't worked. So it seems like she
spent that money on the lawyer for nothing. Everything
just seems to be getting worse. If my father came back
the money problems would be over.

Well, I should close now. This being the third time
I wrote in to nominate my mother for Queen for a Day
and so far not getting any answer, I guess it's safe to say
you don't think her story is sad enough to let her go on
your show. That's okay because there are hundreds of
women in America whose stories are much sadder than
my mom's and they deserve the chance to win some
prizes on your show and be named queen for a day. But
my mom deserves that chance too, just as much as that
lady with the amputated legs I saw and the lady whose
daughter had that rare blood disease and her husband
died last year. My mom needs recognition just as much as
those other ladies need what they need. That's why I
keep writing to you like this. I think this will be my last
letter though. I get the picture, as they say.

Sincerely,

Earl Painter

The Friday before Christmas, Earl, George, Louise, and
their mother are sitting in the darkened living room, George

sprawled on the floor, the others on the sofa, all of them eating popcorn from a bowl held in Louise's lap and watching *The Jackie Gleason Show,* when the phone rings.

"You get it, George," Earl says.

Reggie Van Gleason III swirls his cape and cane across the tiny screen in front of them, and the phone goes on ringing. "Get it yourself," says George. "I always get it and it's never for me."

"Answer the phone, Louise," their mother says, and she suddenly laughs at one of Gleason's moves, a characteristic high-pitched peal that cuts off abruptly, half a cackle that causes her sons, as usual, to look at each other and roll their eyes in shared embarrassment. She's wearing her flannel bathrobe and slippers, smoking a cigarette, and drinking from a glass of beer poured from a quart bottle on the floor beside her.

Crossing in front of them, Louise cuts to the corner table by the window and picks up the phone. Her face, serious most of the time anyhow, suddenly goes dark, then brightens, wide-eyed. Earl watches her, and he knows who she is listening to. She nods, as if the person on the other end can see her, and then she says, "Yes, yes," but no one, except Earl, pays any attention to her.

After a moment, the child puts the receiver down gently and returns to the sofa. "It's Daddy," she announces. "He says he wants to talk to the boys."

"I don't want to talk to him," George blurts, and stares straight ahead at the television.

Their mother blinks, opens and closes her mouth, looks from George to Louise to Earl and back to Louise again. "It's Daddy?" she says. "On the telephone?"

"Uh-huh. He says he wants to talk to the boys."

Earl crosses his arms over his chest and shoves his body back into the sofa. Jackie Gleason dances delicately across the stage, a graceful fat man with a grin.

"Earl?" his mother asks, eyebrows raised.

"Nope."

The woman stands up slowly and walks to the phone. Their mother speaks to their father; all three children watch carefully. She says, "Nelson?" and nods, listening, now and then opening her mouth to say something, closing it when she's interrupted. "Yes, yes," she says, and, "yes, they're both here." She listens again, then says, "Yes, I know, but I should tell you, Nelson, the children . . . the boys, they feel funny about talking to you. Maybe . . . maybe you could write a letter first or something. It's sort of . . . hard for them. They feel very upset, you see, especially now, with the holidays and all. We're all very upset and worried. And with me losing my job and having to work down at Grover Cronin's and all. . . ." She nods, listens, her face expressionless. "Well, Lord knows, that would be very nice. It would have been very nice a long time ago, but no matter. We surely need it, Nelson." She listens again, longer this time, her face gaining energy and focus as she listens. "Yes, yes, I know. Well, I'll see, I'll ask them again. Wait a minute," she says, and puts her hand over the receiver and says, "Earl, your father wants to talk to you. He really does." She smiles wanly.

Earl squirms in his seat, crosses and uncrosses his legs, looks away from his mother to the wall opposite. "I got nothin' to say to him."

"Yes, but . . . I think he wants to say some things to you, though. Can't hurt to let him say them."

Silently, the boy gets up from the couch and crosses the room to the phone. As she hands him the receiver, his mother smiles with a satisfaction that bewilders and instantly angers him.

"H'lo," he says.

"H'lo, son. How're ya doin', boy?"

"Okay."

"Attaboy. Been a while, eh?"

"Yeah. A while."

"Well, I sure am sorry for that, you know, that it's been such a while and all, but I been going through some hard

times myself. Got laid off, didn't work for most of the summer because of that damned strike. You read about that in
the papers?"

"No."

"How's the paper route?"

"Okay."

"Hey, son, look, I know it's been tough for a while, believe me, I know. It's been tough for us all, for everyone. So
I know whatcha been going through. No kidding. But it's
gonna get better, things're gonna be better now. And I want
to try and make it up to you guys a little, what you hadda
go through this last six months or so. I want to make it up
to you guys a little, you and Georgie and Louise. Your ma
too. If you'll let me. Whaddaya say?"

"What?"

"Whaddaya say you let me try to make it up a little to
you?"

"Sure. Why not? Try."

"Hey, listen, Earl, that's quite a attitude you got there.
We got to do something about that, eh? Some kind of attitude, son. I guess things've done a little changing around
there since the old man left, eh? Eh?"

"Sure they have. What'd you expect? Everything'd stay
the same?" Earl hears his voice rising and breaking into a
yodel, and his eyes fill with tears.

"No, of course not. I understand, son. I understand. I
know I've made some big mistakes this year, lately. Especially with you kids, in dealing with you kids. I didn't do it
right, the leaving and all. It's hard, Earl, to do things like that
right. I've learned a lot. But hey, listen, everybody deserves
a second chance. Right? Right? Even your old man?"

"I guess so. Yeah."

"Sure. Damn right," he says, and then he adds that he'd
like to come by tomorrow afternoon and see them, all of
them, and leave off some Christmas presents. "You guys got
your tree yet?"

Earl can manage only a tiny, cracked voice: "No, not yet."

"Well, that's good, real good. 'Cause I already got one in the back of the truck, a eight-footer I cut this afternoon myself. There's lotsa trees out in the woods here in Holderness. Not many people and lotsa trees. Anyhow, I got me a eight-footer, Scotch pine. Them are the best. Whaddaya think?"

"Yeah. Sounds good."

His father rattles on, while Earl feels his chest tighten into a knot, and tears spill over his cheeks. The man repeats several times that he's really sorry about the way he's handled things these last few months, but it's been hard for him, too, and it's hard for him even to say this, he's never been much of a talker, but he knows he's not been much of a father lately, either. That's all over now, though, over and done with, he assures Earl; it's all a part of the past. He's going to be a different man now, a new man. He's turned over a new leaf, he says. And Christmas seems like the perfect time for a new beginning, which is why he called them tonight and why he wants to come by tomorrow afternoon with presents and a tree and help set up and decorate the tree with them, just like in the old days. "Would you go for that? How'd that be, son?"

"Daddy?"

"Yeah, sure, son. What?"

"Daddy, are you gonna try to get back together with Mom?" Earl looks straight at his mother as he says this, and though she pretends to be watching Jackie Gleason, she is listening to his every word, he knows. As is George, and probably even Louise.

"Am I gonna try to get back together with your mom, eh?"

"Yeah."

"Well . . . that's a hard one, boy. You asked me a hard one." He is silent for a few seconds, and Earl can hear him sipping from a glass and then taking a deep draw from his cigarette. "I'll tell ya, boy. The truth is, she don't want me back. You oughta know that by now. I left because *she* wanted me to leave, son. I did some wrong things, sure, lots of 'em, but I did not want to leave you guys. No, right from the beginning, this thing's been your mom's show, not mine."

"Daddy, that's a lie."

"No, son. No. We fought a lot, your mom and me, like married people always do. But I didn't want to leave her and you kids. She told me to. And now, look at this—*she's* the one bringing these divorce charges and all, not me. You oughta see the things she's charging me with."

"What about . . . what about her having to protect herself? You know what I mean. I don't want to go into any details, but you know what I mean. And what about your *girl*-friend?" he sneers.

His father is silent for a moment. Then he says, "You sure have got yourself an attitude since I been gone. Listen, kid, there's lots you don't know anything about, that nobody knows anything about, and there's lots more that you *shouldn't* know anything about. You might not believe this, Earl, but you're still a kid. You're a long ways from being a man. So don't go butting into where you're not wanted and getting into things between your mom and me that you can't understand anyhow. Just butt out. You hear me?"

"Yeah. I hear you."

"Lemme speak to your brother."

"He doesn't want to talk to you," Earl says, and he looks away from George's face and down at his own feet.

"Put your mother on, Earl."

"None of us wants to talk to you."

"Earl!" his mother cries. "Let me have the phone," she says, and she rises from the couch, her hand reaching toward him.

Earl places the receiver in its cradle. Then he stands there, looking into his mother's blue eyes, and she looks into his.

She says, "He won't call back."

Earl says, "I know."

My Mother's Memoirs, My Father's Lie, and Other True Stories

My mother tells me stories about her past, and I don't believe them, I interpret them.

She told me she had the female lead in the Catamount High School senior play and Sonny Tufts had the male lead. She claimed that he asked her to the cast party, but by then she was in love with my father, a stagehand for the play, so she turned down the boy who became a famous movie actor and went to the cast party with the boy who became a New Hampshire carpenter.

She also told me that she knew the principals in Grace Metalious's novel *Peyton Place*. The same night the girl in the book murdered her father, she went afterwards to a Christmas party given by my mother and father in Catamount. "The girl acted strange," my mother said. "Kind of like she was on drugs or something, you know? And the boy she was with, one of the Goldens. He just got drunk and depressed, and then they left. The next day we heard about the police finding the girl's father in the manure pile. . . ."

"Manure pile?"

"She buried him there. And your father told me to keep quiet, not to tell a soul they were at our party on Christmas

Eve. That's why our party isn't in the book or the movie they made of it," she explained.

She also insists, in the face of my repeated denials, that she once saw me being interviewed on television by Dan Rather.

I remembered these three stories recently when, while pawing through a pile of old newspaper clippings, I came upon the obituary of Sonny Tufts. Since my adolescence, I have read two and sometimes three newspapers a day, and frequently I clip an article that for obscure or soon forgotten reasons attracts me; then I toss the clipping into a desk drawer, and every once in a while, without scheduling it, I am moved to read through the clippings and throw them out. It's an experience that fills me with a strange sadness, a kind of grief for my lost self, as if I were reading and throwing out old diaries.

But it's my mother I was speaking of. She grew up poor and beautiful in a New England mill town, Catamount, New Hampshire, the youngest of the five children of a machinist whose wife died ("choked to death on a porkchop bone"— another of her stories) when my mother was nineteen. She was invited the same year, 1933, to the Chicago World's Fair to compete in a beauty pageant but didn't accept the invitation, though she claims my father went to the fair and played his clarinet in a National Guard marching band. Her father, she said, made her stay in Catamount that summer, selling dresses for Grover Cronin's Department Store on River Street. If her mother had not died that year, she would have been able to go to the fair. "And who knows," she joked, "you might've ended up the son of Miss Chicago World's Fair of 1933."

To tell the truth, I don't know very much about my mother's life before 1940, the year I was born and started gathering material for my own stories. Like most people, I pay scant attention to the stories I'm told about lives and events that precede the remarkable event of my own birth. We all seem to tell and hear our own memoirs. It's the same with my children. I watch their adolescent eyes glaze over, their attention drift on to secret plans for the evening and weekend, as I point out the tenement on Perley Street in Catamount where I spent my childhood. Soon it will be too late, I want to say. Soon I, too, will be living in exile, retired from the cold like my mother in San Diego, alone in a drab apartment in a project by the bay, collecting social security and wondering if I'll have enough money at the end of the month for a haircut. Soon all you'll have of me will be your memories of my stories.

Everyone knows that the death of a parent is a terrible thing. But because our parents usually have not been a part of our daily lives for years, most of us do not miss them when they die. When my father died, even though I had been seeing him frequently and talking with him on the phone almost every week, I did not miss him. Yet his death was for me a terrible thing and goes on being a terrible thing now, five years later. My father, a depressed, cynical alcoholic, did not tell stories, but even if he had told stories—about his childhood in Nova Scotia, about beating out Sonny Tufts in the courtship of my mother, about playing the clarinet at the Chicago World's Fair—I would not have listened. No doubt, in his cynicism and despair of ever being loved, he knew that.

The only story my father told me that I listened to closely, visualized, and have remembered, he told me a few months before he died. It was the story of how he came to name me Earl. Naturally, as a child I asked, and he simply shrugged and said he happened to like the name. My mother corroborated the shrug. But one Sunday morning the winter before he died, three years before he planned to retire and move to a trailer down south, I was sitting across from my father in his kitchen, watching him drink tumblers of Canadian Club and ginger ale, and he wagged a finger in my face and told me that I did not know who I was named after.

"I thought no one," I said.

"When I was a kid," he said, "my parents tried to get rid of me in the summers. They used to send me to stay with my uncle Earl up on Cape Breton. He was a bachelor and kind of a hermit, and he stayed drunk most of the time. But he played the fiddle, the violin. And he loved me. He was quite a character. But then, when I was about twelve, I was old enough to spend my summers working, so they kept me down in Halifax after that. And I never saw Uncle Earl again."

He paused and sipped at his drink. He was wearing his striped pajamas and maroon bathrobe and carpet slippers and was chain-smoking Parliaments. His wife (his second—my mother divorced him when I was twelve, because of his drinking and what went with it) had gone to the market as soon as I arrived, as if afraid to leave him without someone else in the house. "He died a few years later," my father said. "Fell into a snowbank, I heard. Passed out. Froze to death."

I listened to the story and have remembered it today because I thought it was about *me*, my name, Earl. My father told it, of course, because it was about *him*, and because for an instant that cold February morning he dared to hope that his oldest son would love him.

At this moment, as I say this, I do love him, but it's too late for the saying to make either of us happy. That is why I say the death of a parent is a terrible thing.

After my father died, I asked his sister Ethel about poor old Uncle Earl. She said she never heard of the man. The unofficial family archivist and only a few years younger than my father, she surely would have known of him, would have known how my father spent his summers, would have

known of the man he loved enough to name his firstborn son
after.

The story simply was not true. My father had made it up.

Just as my mother's story about Sonny Tufts is not true.
Yesterday, when I happened to come across the article about
Sonny Tufts from the *Boston Globe,* dated June 8, 1970, and
written by the late George Frazier, I wouldn't have both-
ered to reread it if the week before I had not been joking
about Sonny Tufts with a friend, a woman who lives in Boston and whose mother died this past summer. My friend's
mother's death, like my father's, was caused by acute alcoholism and had been going on for years. What most suicides
accomplish in minutes, my father and my friend's mother
took decades to do.

The death of my friend's mother reminded me of the
consequences of the death of my father and of my mother's
continuing to live. And then our chic joke about the 1940s
film star ("Whatever happened to Sonny Tufts?"), a joke
about our own aging, reminded me of my mother's story
about the senior play in 1932, so that when I saw Frazier's
obituary for Tufts, entitled "Death of a Bonesman" (Tufts
had gone to Yale and been tapped for Skull and Bones), instead of tossing it back in the drawer or into the wastebasket,
I read it through to the end, as if searching for a reference
to my mother's having brushed him off. Instead, I learned
that Bowen Charlton Tufts III, scion of an old Boston bank-
ing family, had prepped for Yale at Exeter. So that his closest
connection to the daughter of a machinist in Catamount, and
to me, was probably through his father's bank's ownership
of the mill where the machinist ran a lathe.

I had never believed the story anyhow, but now I had
proof that she made it up. Just as the fact that I have never
been interviewed by Dan Rather is proof that my mother
never saw me on television in her one-room apartment in
San Diego being interviewed by Dan Rather. By the time

she got her friend down the hall to come and see her son on TV, Dan had gone on to some depressing stuff about the Middle East.

As for Grace Metalious's characters from *Peyton Place* showing up at a Christmas party in my parents' house in Catamount, I never believed that, either. *Peyton Place* was indeed based on a true story about a young woman's murder of her father in Gilmanton, New Hampshire, a village some twenty-five miles from Catamount, but in the middle 1940s people simply did not drive twenty-five miles over snow-covered back roads on a winter night to go to a party given by strangers.

I said that to my mother. She had just finished telling me, for the hundredth time, it seemed, that someday, based on my own experiences as a child and now as an adult in New Hampshire, I should be able to write another *Peyton Place.* This was barely two months ago, and I was visiting her in San Diego, an extension of a business trip to Los Angeles, and I was seated rather uncomfortably in her one-room apartment. She is a tiny, wrenlike woman with few possessions, most of which seem miniaturized, designed to fit her small body and the close confines of her room, so that when I visit her I feel huge and oafish. I lower my voice and move with great care.

She was ironing her sheets, while I sat on the unmade sofa bed, unmade because I had just turned the mattress for her, a chore she saves for when I or my younger brother, the only large-sized people in her life now, visits her from the East. "But we *weren't* strangers to them," my mother chirped. "Your father knew the Golden boy somehow. Probably one of his local drinking friends," she said. "Anyhow, that's why your father wouldn't let me tell anyone, after the story came out in the papers, about the murder and the incest and all. . . ."

"Incest? What incest?"

"You know, the father who got killed, killed and buried

in the manure pile by his own daughter because he'd been committing incest with her. Didn't you read the book?"

"No."

"Well, your father, he was afraid we'd get involved somehow. So I couldn't tell anyone about it until after the book got famous. You know, whenever I tell people out here that back in New Hampshire in the forties I knew the girl who killed her father in *Peyton Place,* they won't believe me. Well, not exactly *knew* her, but you know. . . ."

There's always someone famous in her stories, I thought. Dan Rather, Sonny Tufts, Grace Metalious (though my mother can never remember her name, only the name of the book she wrote). It's as if she hopes you will love her more easily if she is associated somehow with fame.

When you know a story isn't true, you think you don't have to listen to it. What you think you're supposed to do is interpret, as I was doing that morning in my mother's room, converting her story into a clue to her psychology, which in turn would lead me to compare it to my own psychology and, with relief, disapprove. (*My* stories don't have famous people in them.) I did the same thing with my father's drunken fiddler, Uncle Earl, once I learned he didn't exist. I used the story as a clue to help unravel the puzzle of my father's dreadful psychology, hoping no doubt to unravel the puzzle of my own.

One of the most difficult things to say to another person is I hope you will love me. Yet that is what we all want to say to one another—to our children, to our parents and mates, to our friends and even to strangers.

Perhaps especially to strangers. My friend in Boston, who joked with me about Sonny Tufts as an interlude in the story of her mother's awful dying, was showing me her hope that I would love her, even when the story itself was about her mother's lifelong refusal to love her and, with the woman's death, the absolute removal of any possibility of that love. I have, at least, my father's story of how I got my name, and

though it's too late for me now to give him what, for a glim-
mering moment, he hoped and asked for, by remembering
his story I have understood a little more usefully the telling
of my own.

By remembering, as if writing my memoirs, what the stories of others have reminded me of, what they have literally
brought to my mind, I have learned how my own stories
function in the world, whether I tell them to my mother, to
my wife, to my children, to my friends or, especially, to
strangers. And to complete the circle, I have learned a little
more usefully how to listen to the stories of others, whether
they are true or not.

As I was leaving my mother that morning to drive back
to Los Angeles and then fly home to New Hampshire, where
my brother and sister and all my mother's grandchildren live
and where all but the last few years of my mother's past was
lived, she told me a new story. We stood in the shade of palm
trees in the parking lot outside her glass-and-metal building
for a few minutes, and she said to me in a concerned way,
"You know that restaurant, the Pancake House, where you
took me for breakfast this morning?"

I said yes and checked the time and flipped my suitcase
into the back seat of the rented car.

"Well, I always have breakfast there on Wednesdays, it's
on the way to where I baby-sit on Wednesdays, and this week
something funny happened there. I sat alone way in the
back, where they have that long, curving booth, and I didn't
notice until I was halfway through my breakfast that at the
far end of the booth a man was sitting there. He was maybe
your age, a young man, but dirty and shabby. Especially
dirty, and so I just looked away and went on eating my eggs
and toast.

"But then I noticed he was looking at me, as if he knew
me and didn't quite dare talk to me. I smiled, because maybe
I did know him, I know just about everybody in the neigh-

borhood now. But he was a stranger. And dirty. And I could see that he had been drinking for days.

"So I smiled and said to him, 'You want help, mister, don't you?' He needed a shave, and his clothes were filthy and all ripped, and his hair was a mess. You know the type. But something pathetic about his eyes made me want to talk to him. But honestly, Earl, I couldn't. I just couldn't. He was so dirty and all.

"Anyhow, when I spoke to him, just that little bit, he sort of came out of his daze and sat up straight for a second, like he was afraid I was going to complain to the manager and have him thrown out of the restaurant. 'What did you say to me?' he asked. His voice was weak but he was trying to make it sound strong, so it came out kind of loud and broken. 'Nothing,' I said, and I turned away from him and quickly finished my breakfast and left.

"That afternoon, when I was walking back home from my baby-sitting job, I went into the restaurant to see if he was there, but he wasn't. And the next morning, Thursday, I walked all the way over there to check again, even though I never eat breakfast at the Pancake House on Thursdays, but he was gone then too. And then yesterday, Friday, I went back a third time. But he was gone." She lapsed into a thoughtful silence and looked at her hands.

"Was he there this morning?" I asked, thinking coincidence was somehow the point of the story.

"No," she said. "But I didn't expect him to be there this morning. I'd stopped looking for him by yesterday."

"Well, why'd you tell me the story, then? What's it about?"

"About? Why, I don't know. Nothing, I guess. I just felt sorry for the man, and then because I was afraid, I shut up and left him alone." She was still studying her tiny hands.

"That's natural," I said. "You shouldn't feel guilty for that," I said, and I put my arms around her.

She turned her face into my shoulder. "I know, I know. But still . . ." Her blue eyes filled, her son was leaving again, gone for another six months or a year, and who would she tell her stories to while he was gone? Who would listen?

The
Fish

>————————•——

When Colonel Tung's first attempt to destroy the fish failed, everyone, even the Buddhists, was astonished. On the colonel's orders, a company of soldiers under the command of a young lieutenant named Han marched out from the village early one summer morning as far as the bridge. Departing from the road there, the soldiers made their way in single file through the bamboo groves and shreds of golden mist to a clearing, where they stepped with care over spongy ground to the very edge of the pond, which was then the size of a soccer field. Aiming automatic weapons into the water, the troopers waited for the fish to arrive. A large crowd from the village gathered behind them and, since most of the people were Buddhists, fretted and scowled at the soldiers, saying, "Shame! Shame!" Even some Catholics from the village joined the scolding, though it had been their complaints that first had drawn the colonel's attention to the existence of the huge fish and had obliged him to attempt to destroy it, for pilgrimages to view the fish had come to seem like acts of opposition to his administration. In great numbers, the Buddhists from other districts were visiting the Buddhists in his district, sleeping in local homes, buying food from local vendors, and trading goods of various kinds, until it had begun to seem to Colonel Tung that there were many more Buddhists in his district than Catholics, and this frightened him. Thus his opinion that the pilgrimages to view the fish were acts of political opposition, and thus his determination to destroy the fish.

Shortly after the soldiers lined up at the shore, the fish broke the surface of the water halfway across the pond. It was a silver swirl in the morning sun, a clean swash of movement, like a single brushstroke, for the fish was thought to be a reincarnation of Rad, the painter, an early disciple of Buddha. The soldiers readied their weapons. Lieutenant Han repeated his order: "Wait until I say to fire," he said, and there was a second swirl, a lovely arc of silver bubbles, closer to shore this time. The crowd had gone silent. Many were moving their lips in prayer; all were straining to see over and around the line of soldiers at the shore. Then there it was, a few feet out and hovering in the water like a cloud in the sky, one large dark eye watching the soldiers as if with curiosity, delicate fins fluttering gently in the dark water like translucent leaves. "Fire!" the lieutenant cried. The soldiers obeyed, and their weapons roared for what seemed a long time. The pond erupted and boiled in white fury, and when finally the water was still once again, everyone in the crowd rushed to the shore and searched for the remains of the fish. Even the lieutenant and his band of soldiers pushed to the mud at the edge of the water and looked for the fish, or what everyone thought would be chunks of the fish floating on the still surface of the pond. But they saw nothing, not a scrap of it, until they noticed halfway across the pond a swelling in the water, and the fish rolled and dove, sending a wave sweeping in to shore, where the crowd cried out joyfully and the soldiers and the young lieutenant cursed, for they knew that Colonel Tung was not going to like this, not at all.

They were correct. Colonel Tung took off his sunglasses and glared at the lieutenant, then turned in his chair to face the electric fan for a moment. Finally, replacing his glasses, he said, "Let us assume that in that pond an enemy submarine is surfacing at night to send spies and saboteurs into our midst. Do you have the means to destroy it?" He tapped a cigarette into an ebony holder and lighted it. The lieutenant, like the colonel a man trained at the academy but rapidly adapting his skills to life in the provinces, said yes, he could destroy such an enemy. He would mine the pond, he said, and detonate the mines from shore. "Indeed," the colonel said. "That sounds like a fine idea," and he went back to work.

From a rowboat, the soldiers placed in the pond ten pie-sized mines connected by insulated wires to one another and to a detonator and battery, and when everything was ready and the area had been cleared of civilians, Lieutenant Han set off the detonator from behind a mound of earth they had heaped up for this purpose. There was a deep, convulsive rumble and the surface of the pond blew off, causing a wet wind that had the strength of a gale and tore leaves from the trees and bent the bamboo stalks to the ground. Immediately after the explosion, everyone from the village who was not already at the site rushed to the pond and joined the throng that encircled it. Everything that had ever lived in or near the pond seemed to be dead and floating on its surface—carp, crayfish, smelts, catfish, eels, tortoises, frogs, egrets, woodcocks, peccaries, snakes, feral dogs, lizards, doves, shellfish and all the plants from the bottom, the long grasses, weeds, and reeds, and the banyans, mangroves and other trees rooted in the water and the flowering bushes and the lilies that had floated on the surface of the pond— everything once alive seemed dead. Many people wept openly, some prayed, burned incense, chanted, and others, more practical, rushed about with baskets, gathering up the unexpected harvest. The lieutenant and his soldiers walked intently around the pond, searching for the giant fish. When they could not find it, they rowed out to the middle of the pond and searched there. But still, amongst the hundreds of dead fish and plants, birds and animals floating in the water, they saw no huge silver fish, no carcass that could justify such carnage. Then, as they began to row back toward shore, the lieutenant, who was standing at the bow, his hand shading his eyes from the milky glare of the water, saw before them once again the rolling, shiny side of the giant fish, its dorsal fin like a black knife slicing obliquely across their bow, when it disappeared, only to reappear off the stern a ways, swerving back and suddenly heading straight at the small, crowded boat. The men shouted in fear, and at the last possible second the fish looped back and dove into the dark waters below. The crowd at the shore had seen it, and a great cheer went up, and in seconds there were drums and cymbals and all kinds of song joining the cheers, as the soldiers rowed slowly, glumly, in to shore.

The reputation of the fish and its miraculous powers began to spread rapidly across the whole country, and great flocks of believers undertook pilgrimages to the pond, where they set up tents and booths on the shore. Soon the settlement surrounding the pond was as large as the village where the colonel's district headquarters was located. Naturally, this alarmed the colonel, for these pilgrims were Buddhists, many of them fanatics, and he, a Catholic, was no longer sure he could rule them. "We must destroy that fish," he said to the lieutenant, who suggested this time that he and his soldiers pretend to join the believers and scatter pieces of bread over the waters to feed the fish, as had become the custom. They would do this from the boat, he said, and with specially sweetened chunks of bread, and when the fish was used to being fed this way and approached the boat carelessly close, they would lob hand grenades painted white as bread into the water, and the fish, deceived, would swallow one or two or more whole, as it did the bread, and that would be that. Colonel Tung admired the plan and sent his man off to implement it instantly. Lieutenant Han's inventive-

ness surprised the colonel and pleased him, though he fore-
saw problems, for if the plan worked, he would be obliged
to promote the man, which would place Han in a position
where he could begin to covet his superior's position as district commander. This damned fish, the colonel said to himself, may be the worst thing to happen to me.

It soon appeared that Lieutenant Han's plan was working, for the fish, which seemed recently to have grown to an
even more gigantic size than before and was now almost
twice the size of the boat, approached the boat without fear
and rubbed affectionately against it, or so it seemed, whenever the soldiers rowed out to the middle of the pond and
scattered large chunks of bread, which they did twice a day.
Each time, the fish gobbled the chunks, cleared the water
entirely and swam rapidly away. The throng on shore
cheered, for they, too, had taken the bait—they believed
that the soldiers, under the colonel's orders, had come to ap-
preciate the fish's value to the district as a whole, to Catholics
as much as to Buddhists, for everyone, it seemed, was profit-
ing from its presence—tentmakers, carpenters, farmers,
storekeepers, clothiers, woodchoppers, scribes, entrepre-
neurs of all types, entertainers, even, musicians and jugglers,
and of course the manufacturers of altars and religious images and also of paintings and screens purported to have
been made by the original Rad, the artist and early disciple
of Buddha, now reincarnated as the giant fish.

When finally Lieutenant Han gave the order to float the
specially prepared grenades out with the bread, several soldiers balked. They had no objections to blowing up the fish,
but they were alarmed by the size of the crowd now more
or less residing on the shore and, as usual, watching them
in hopes of seeing the fish surface to feed. "If this time we
succeed in destroying the fish," a soldier said, "the people
may not let us get back to shore. There are now thousands
of them, Catholics as well as Buddhists, and but ten of us."
The lieutenant pointed out that the crowd had no weapons

and they had automatic rifles that could easily clear a path from the shore to the road and back to the village. "And once the fish is gone, the people will go away, and things will settle back into their normal ways again." The soldiers took heart and proceeded to drop the grenades into the water with an equal number of chunks of bread. The fish, large as a house, had been lurking peacefully off the stern of the boat and now swept past, swooping up all the bread and the grenades in one huge swallow. It turned away and rolled, exposing its silver belly to the sun, as if in gratitude, and the crowd cried out in pleasure. The music rose, with drums, cymbals, flutes joining happily and floating to the sky on swirling clouds of incense, while the soldiers rowed furiously for shore. The boat scraped gravel, and the troopers jumped out, dragged the boat up onto the mud and made their way quickly through the throng toward the road. As they reached the road, they heard the first of the explosions, then the others in rapid succession, a tangled knot of bangs as all the grenades went off, in the air, it seemed, out of the water and certainly not inside the fish's belly. It was as if the fish were spitting the grenades out just as they were about to explode, creating the effect of a fireworks display above the pond, which must have been what caused the people gathered at the shore to break into sustained, awestruck applause and then, long into the day and the following night, song.

Now the reputation of the miraculous fish grew tenfold, and busloads of pilgrims began to arrive from as far away as Saigon and Bangkok. People on bicycles, on donkeys, in trucks and in oxcarts made their way down the dusty road from the village to the pond, where as many of them as could find a spot got down to the shore and prayed to the fish for help, usually against disease and injury, for the fish was thought to be especially effective in this way. Some prayed for wealth or for success in love or for revenge against their enemies, but these requests were not thought likely to be answered, though it surely did no harm to try. Most of those

who came now took away with them containers filled with
water from the pond. They arrived bearing bowls, buckets,
fruit tins, jars, gourds, even cups, and they took the water
with them back to their homes in the far corners of the country, where many of them were able to sell off small vials of
the water for surprisingly high prices to those unfortunate
neighbors and loved ones unable to make the long overland
journey to the pond. Soldiers, too, whenever they passed
through Colonel Tung's district, came to the pond and filled
their canteens with the magical waters. More than once a
helicopter landed on the shore, and a troop of soldiers
jumped out, ran to the pond, filled their canteens and returned to the helicopter and took off again. Thus, when Lieutenant Han proposed to Colonel Tung that this time they try
to destroy the fish by poisoning the water in the pond, the
colonel demurred. "I think that instead of trying to kill the
fish, we learn how to profit from it ourselves. It's too dangerous now," he observed, "to risk offending the people by taking away what has become their main source of income.
What I have in mind, my boy, is a levy, a tax on the water
that is taken away from this district. A modest levy, not
enough to discourage the pilgrims, but more than enough
to warrant the efforts and costs of collection." The colonel
smiled slyly and set his lieutenant to the task. There will be
no promotions now, he said to himself, for there are no hero-
ics in tax collecting.

And so a sort of calm and orderliness settled over the district, which pleased everyone, Colonel Tung most of all, but
also Lieutenant Han, who managed to collect the tax on the
water so effectively that he was able without detection to cut
a small percentage out of it for himself, and the soldiers, who
felt much safer collecting taxes than trying to destroy a miraculous and beloved fish, and the people themselves, who,
because they now paid a fee for the privilege of taking away
a container of pond water, no longer doubted the water's

magical power to cure illness and injury, to let the blind see, the lame walk, the deaf hear, the dumb talk. The summer turned into fall, the fall became winter, and there were no changes in the district, until the spring, when it became obvious to everyone that the pond was much smaller in diameter than it had been in previous springs. The summer rains that year were heavy, though not unusually so, and the colonel hoped that afterwards the pond would be as large as before, but it was not. In September, when the dry season began, the colonel tried to restrict the quantity of water taken from the pond. This proved impossible, for by now too many people had too many reasons to keep on taking water away. A powerful black market operated in several cities, and at night tanker trucks edged down to the shore, where they sucked thousands of gallons of water out, and the next morning the surface of the pond would be yet another foot lower than before and encircling it would be yet another mud aureole inside the old shoreline.

At last there came the morning when the pond was barely large enough to hold the fish. The colonel, wearing sunglasses, white scarf, and cigarette holder, and Lieutenant Han and the soldiers and many of the pilgrims walked across the drying mud to the edge of the water, where they lined up around the tiny pool, little more than a puddle now, and examined the fish. It lay on its side, half exposed to the sun. One gill, blood-red inside, opened and closed, but no water ran through. One eye was above water, one below, and the eye above was clouded over and fading to white. A pilgrim who happened to be carrying a pail leaned down, filled his pail and splashed the water over the side of the fish. Another pilgrim with a gourd joined him, and two soldiers went back to the encampment and returned with a dozen containers of various types and sizes, which they distributed to the others, even including the colonel. Soon everyone was dipping his container into the water and splashing it over the silvery side of the huge, still fish. By midday, however, the sun had evaporated most of the water, and the containers were filled with more mud than moisture, and by sunset they had buried the fish.

Success
Story

After high school, I attended an Ivy League college for less than one term. A year later, I was married and living in central Florida. This was 1958 and '59. General Dwight Eisenhower was our President, and Dr. Fidel Castro, hunkered down in the mountain passes southeast of Havana, was getting praised for his integrity and good looks by *Time* and *Reader's Digest.*

I'd been a whiz kid in high school, rewarded for it with an academic scholarship as fat as the starting quarterback's at a midwestern state university. In this Ivy League school, however, among the elegant, brutal sons of the captains of industry, I was only that year's token poor kid, imported from a small New Hampshire mill town like an exotic herb, a dash of mace for the vichyssoise. It was a status that perplexed and intimidated and finally defeated me, so that, after nine weeks of it, I fled in the night.

Literally. On a snowy December night, alone in my dormitory room (they had not thought it appropriate for me to have a roommate, or no one's profile matched mine), I packed my clothes and few books into a canvas duffel, waited until nearly all the lights on campus were out and sneaked down the hallway, passed through the service entrance and walked straight down the hill from the eighteenth-century brick dormitories and classroom buildings to the wide boulevard below, where huge, neoclassical fraternity houses lounged beneath high, ancient elms. At the foot of the hill, I turned south and jogged through unplowed snow, shifting my heavy duffel from one shoulder to the other every twenty or thirty yards, until I passed out of the valley town into darkness and found myself walking through a heavy snowstorm on a winding, narrow road.

A month later, with the holidays over and my distraught mother and bewildered younger brother and sister, aunts, uncles, and cousins, all my friends and neighbors and high school teachers, as well as the director of admissions at the Ivy League college, convinced that I not only had ruined my life but may have done something terrible to theirs, too, I turned up in St. Petersburg, Florida, with seven dollars in my pocket, my duffel on my shoulder and my resolve to join Castro in the Sierra Maestra seriously weakening.

I'd spent Christmas and New Year's at home, working days and nights as a salesman in a local men's clothing store and trying hard to behave as if nothing had happened. My mother seemed always to be red-eyed from weeping, and my friends from high school treated me coolly, distantly, as if I had dropped out of college because of a social disease. In some ways, my family was a civic reclamation project—the bright and pretty children and pathetic wife of a brute who, nearly a decade ago, had disappeared into the northern woods with a woman from the post office, never to be heard from again. As the oldest male victim of this abandonment, I was expected by everyone who knew the story to avenge the crime, mainly by making myself visibly successful, by rising above my station and in that paradoxical way showing the criminal how meaningless his crime had been. For reasons I was only dimly aware of, my story was important to everyone.

Leaving them behind, then, abandoning my fatherless family in a tenement and my old friends and the town I had been raised in, was an exquisite pleasure, like falling into bed and deep sleep after having been pushed beyond exhaustion. Now, I thought the morning I left—stepping onto the ramp to Route 93 in Catamount, showing my thumb to the cars headed south—*now* I can start to dream my own dreams, not everyone else's.

The particular dream of joining Castro died easily. It started dying the moment I got out of the big, blue Buick sedan with Maryland plates that had carted me straight through all the way from Norfolk, Virginia, to Coquina Key in St. Petersburg, where the elderly man who drove the car had a "girlfriend," he told me, who had a suite in the Coquina Key Hotel.

"You, you're a smart kid," he said to me, as I slid from the car and hauled out my duffel from the back. "You'll do all right here. You'll catch on." He was a ruddy, white-haired man with a brush cut that he liked to touch with the flat of his hand, as if patting a strange dog. "Forget Cuba, though. No sense getting yourself killed for somebody else's country." He was a retired U.S. Army captain, named Heinz, "like the ketchup," he'd said, and he gave advice as if he expected it to be taken. "Kid like you," he said, peering across at me from the driver's seat, "smart, good-looking, good personality, you can make a million bucks here. This place," he said, looking warmly around him at the marina, the palm trees, the acres of lawn, the flashy bougainvillea blossoms, the large new cars with out-of-state plates, the tall, pink Coquina Key Hotel with the dark red canopy leading from the street to the front entrance, "this place is *made* for a kid like you."

"Yeah. Well, I got plenty of time for that." I took a step

away from the car, and Heinz leaned farther across the front
seat to see me. I said to him, "I don't need to make a pile
of money just yet."

"No? How much you got?"

"Not much. Enough." I lifted my duffel to my shoulder
and gave the man a wave.

"If you don't need money, kid, what *do* you need, then?"

"Experience, I guess." I tried to smile knowingly.

"Listen. I been coming down here every goddamned
winter for eight years now, ever since I retired. I *got* experience, and lemme tell you, this place is gonna be a boom
town. It already is. All these old people from the north, and
there's gonna be more of 'em, kid, not less, and all of 'em
got money to spend, and here you are on the ground floor.
I'd give all my experience for your youth. Kid, forget Cuba.
Stay in St. Pete and you'll be a millionaire before you're
twenty-five."

I was sorry now that I'd told Heinz the truth back in Virginia, when he'd asked me where I was going. I'd said Cuba,
and he'd laughed and asked why, and I had tried to tell him,
but all I could say was that I wanted to help the Cuban people liberate themselves from a cruel and corrupt dictator.
We both knew how that sounded, and neither of us had spoken of Cuba again, until now.

I stepped away from the car to the curb. "Well, thanks.
Thanks for the advice. And the ride. Good meeting you," I
said.

He called me by my name. I hadn't thought he'd caught
it. "Look, if you need some help," he said to me, "just give
me a call," and he stuck his hand with a small white card out
the window on the passenger's side.

I took the card and read his first name, Harry, his address
back in Chevy Chase, Maryland, and a post office box here
in St. Petersburg. "Thanks," I said.

"I stay at the hotel," Heinz said, nodding toward the high
pink stuccoed building. "With my girlfriend. Her name's

Sturgis, Bea Sturgis, she's here all the time, year round. Nice woman. Give a call anytime."

"I'm okay," I said. "Really. I know what I'm doing."

He smiled. "No," he said. "You don't." Then he waved goodbye, dropped the Buick into gear and moved off slowly toward the hotel garage.

It was not quite nine in the morning, and it was already hot. I peeled off my jacket, tied it to the duffel and strolled across the street to the park by the marina and sat down on a bench facing the street. Behind me, charter fishing boats and yachts rocked tenderly against the narrow dock, where pelicans perched somberly on the bollards. Across the street, men and women in short-sleeved, pastel-colored blouses and shirts and plaid Bermuda shorts drifted in and out of the hotel. New cars and taxis and limousines drove people by and let people off and picked people up. A light breeze riffled quietly through the royal palm trees that lined the street. Everyone and everything belonged exactly where it was.

I was suddenly hungry and realized that I hadn't eaten since the night before at a Stuckey's in North Carolina. A few minutes passed, and then I saw Heinz emerge from the parking garage at the left of the hotel and walk briskly along the sidewalk toward the hotel, his gaze straight ahead of him, businesslike. He reached the canopy, turned under it, and entered the building, nodding agreeably to the doorman as he passed through the glass doors to the dark, cool interior.

I stood up slowly, grabbed my duffel, crossed the street, and followed him.

I never saw Heinz again, however. I called him from the house phone in the lobby, and he laughed and called the manager, who met me at the front desk and gave me a note to take to the concierge, who put me to work that very day as a furniture mover.

I was the youngest and the healthiest of a gang of seven

or eight men who set up tables and chairs for meeting rooms and convention halls, decorated ballrooms for wedding receptions, moved pianos from one dining room to another, dragged king-sized mattresses from suite to suite, unloaded supplies from trucks, delivered carts of dirty linen to the basement laundry, lugged sofas, lamps, cribs and carpets from one end of the hotel to the other. Paid less than thirty dollars a week for six ten-hour days a week, we worked staggered shifts and were on call seven days a week, twenty-four hours a day. We were given room and board and ate in a bare room off the hotel kitchen with the dishwashers and slept two to a tiny, cell-like room in a cinder-block dormitory behind the hotel.

Most of the kitchen help was black and went home, or somewhere, at night. We furniture movers were to a man white and, except for me, over forty, terminally alcoholic, physically fragile and itinerant. It took me a few days to realize that we were all a type of migrant worker, vagrants, wanderers down from the cold cities and railroad yards of the north, and that the day after payday most of this week's crew would be gone, replaced the next day by a new group of men, who, a week later, would leave, too, for Miami, New Orleans or Los Angeles. No one else wanted our jobs, and we couldn't get any other. We were underpaid, overworked and looked down upon by chambermaids, elevator operators and doormen. Like certain plumbing tools, we were not thought to exist until we were needed.

Even so, less than two weeks into this line of work, I decided to succeed at it. Which was like deciding to succeed at being a prisoner of war, deciding to become a *good* prisoner of war. I believed that I could become so good at moving furniture that I'd be irreplaceable and shortly thereafter would be made boss of the furniture movers, and then my talent for organization, my affection for the hotel and the warmth of my personality would be recognized by the concierge, who would promote me, would make me his assistant, say, and from there I'd go on to concierge itself, then assistant manager, until, before long, why not manager? In the distant future, I saw a chain of hotels linking every major city on the Gulf of Mexico (a body of water I had not actually seen yet) that I would control from a bank of telephones here on my desk in St. Petersburg at the Coquina Key, which, since it was where I got my start, would become the central jewel in my necklace of hotels and resorts, my diadem, a modest man's point of understandable pride. I would entertain world leaders here—Dr. Fidel Castro, President Dwight Eisenhower, Generalissimo Chiang Kai Shek. People would congratulate me for having dropped out of an Ivy League college after less than one term, and my mother and brother and sister would now realize the wisdom of my decision, and friends from high school would call me up, begging for jobs in my hotels. Late at night, lying in my narrow bunk, my temporary roommate snoring in the bunk below, I imagined testimonial dinners at which I would single out my old friend Heinz from Chevy Chase. He'd be seated alongside his lady, Bea Sturgis, at the head table, just beyond the mayor of St. Petersburg and the governor of Florida. "It all started with Heinz" I'd say. "He told me this place was made for a guy like me, and he was right!"

Furniture movers came and went, but I stayed. The fourth person in five weeks with whom I shared my grim cell was named Bob O'Neil, from Chicago, and when he found out that I'd been a furniture mover at the Coquina Key for longer than a month now, he told me I was crazy. I'd come back from setting up a VFW luncheon in the Oleander Room, hoping to sneak a few hours' sleep, as I'd been up most of the night before, taking down the tables and chairs and cleaning up the hall after an all-state sports award banquet. My previous roommate, Fred from Columbus, a fat, morosely silent man whose hands trembled while he read religious tracts which he worldlessly passed on to me, had got his first week's pay two days before and had taken off, for Phoenix, he said, where his sister lived.

My new roommate, when I arrived, had already claimed

the bottom bunk—mine, I had decided, after Fred left—and had removed my magazines and was now lying stretched out on it. I closed the door, and he sat up, stuck out his hand and introduced himself.

"Hi," he said. "I'm Bob, and I'm an alcoholic." He was in his early or late forties; it was hard to tell. His face was broad and blotched, with broken veins crisscrossing his cheeks and large red nose. He was bright-eyed and had a cheerful, loose mouth and a wash of thin, sandy-gray hair.

I removed his open, nearly empty, cardboard suitcase from the only chair in the room and sat down. I said, "How come you tell people you're an alcoholic?" and he explained that he was required to by Alcoholics Anonymous, which he said he had joined the day before.

"That's what you *got* to say," he said. "You got to admit to the world that you're an alcoholic. Put it right out there. First step to recovery."

"How long before you're cured?" I asked. "You know, and don't have to go around introducing yourself like that."

"Never," he said. "Never. It's like . . . a condition. Like diabetes, or your height. I'm allergic to booze, to alcohol. Simple as that."

"So you can't touch the stuff?"

"Right. Not unless I want to die." He swung his feet around to the floor and lighted a cigarette. "Smoke?"

"No, thanks. Say," I said, "the bottom bunk's mine."

"You're kidding me," he said, smiling broadly. "Look at you—what're you, eighteen? Twenty?"

"Eighteen. Almost nineteen."

"Eighteen. And here I am, an old, sick man, an alcoholic, and you can jump up there like a pole vaulter. And you're saying that bottom bunk's yours." He sighed, coughed, lay back down and closed his eyes. "All right. It's yours."

"No, go ahead. I'll sleep on top."

"No, no, no! You're right, you got here before me. First come, first served, that's the law of the land. I understand."

I climbed up the rickety ladder at the end of the bunk and flung myself face-forward onto the bed.

"You sure you don't mind?" he asked, sticking his head out and peering up at me.

"No."

"How long you been here, anyhow?"

"Little over five weeks," I said, and thought, Over half as long as I went to college.

"Five weeks!" He laughed. That's when he told me I was crazy, said it in a high, amused voice. "Well," he said, yawning, "you must be getting real good at it."

"Yeah."

Nobody worked these jobs more than a week or at the most two, he explained. "You're like a prisoner, never see the light of day, never make enough money to make a difference in your life, so what you gotta do, you just gotta get your pay and leave. Get the hell out. Find a place or a job that *does* make a difference. Smart, good-looking kid like you," he said, "you can do better than this. This is America, for Christ's sake. You can do real good for yourself. How much money you got saved up?"

"Not much. Little over sixty bucks."

"Well, there you go," he said, as if presenting a self-evident truth.

I thanked him for the advice, explained that I was tired and needed sleep. I was on the night shift that week and had been told to fill in for a guy who'd left the morning crew, something that was happening with increasing frequency, which I had taken as a sure sign of my imminent success. Bob said nothing more, and soon I was asleep.

Over the next few days, whenever we talked, which was often, as he was garrulous and I was lonely, we talked about Bob's alcoholism and my refusal to take his advice, which was to leave the hotel immediately, rent a room in town, get a job in a restaurant or a store, where people could see me, as Bob explained, because, according to him, I had the kind of face people trusted. "An *honest* face," he said, as if it communicated more than merely a commitment to telling the truth, as if intelligence, reliability, sensitivity, personal cleanliness and high ambition all went with it. "You got an *honest* face, kid. You should get the hell out there in the real world, where you can *use* it."

For my part, I advised him to keep going to his AA meetings, which he said he did. He was tempted daily to drink, I knew, by the flask-toters in our crew, and often he'd come into the room trembling, on the verge of tears, and he'd grab me by the shoulders and beg me not to let him do it. "Don't let me give in, kid! Don't let the bastards get to me. Talk to me, kid," he'd beg, and I'd talk to him, remind him of all he'd told me—his broken marriages, his lost jobs, his penniless wanderings between Florida and Chicago, his waking up sick in filthy flophouses and panhandling on street corners—until at last he'd calm down and feel a new determination to resist temptation. I could see that it was hard on him physically. He seemed to be losing weight, and his skin, despite the red blotches and broken veins, had taken on a dull gray pallor, and he never seemed to sleep. We were both on the night shift that week, and all day long, except when he went out for what he said were his AA meetings, I'd hear him in the bunk below, tossing his body from side to side in the dim afternoon light as he struggled to fall asleep, eventually giving up, lighting a cigarette, going out for a walk, returning to try and fail again.

One afternoon, a few days before his first payday, he reached up to my bunk and woke me. "Listen, kid, I can't sleep. Loan me a couple bucks, willya? I got to go get a bottle." His voice was unusually firm, clear. He'd made a decision.

"Bob, don't. You don't want that. Stick it out."

"Don't lecture me, just loan me a coupla bucks." This time he was giving me an order, no request.

I looked into his eyes for a few seconds and saw my own

eyes staring back. "No," I said, and I turned over and went defiantly back to sleep.

When I woke, it was growing dark, and I knew I'd almost missed supper, so I rushed from the room and down the long tunnel that connected the dormitory to the hotel kitchen, where the night dishwashers and furniture movers were already eating. Bob wasn't there, and no one had seen him.

"He's working tonight!" I said. "He's got to work tonight!"

They shrugged and went on eating. No one cared.

A half-dozen rooms on the fourteenth floor were being painted, and we spent the night moving furniture out and storing it in the basement, and there was a chamber of commerce breakfast that we had to set up in the Crepe Myrtle Room, and it was daylight by the time I got back to my room. Bob was there, sound asleep in the bottom bunk.

I looked around the room, checked the tin trash can, even peered into the dresser drawers, but found no bottle. He heard me and rolled over and watched.

"Lookin' for something?"

"You know what."

"A bottle?"

"Yeah. Sure."

"Sorry, kid."

"You didn't drink?"

"Nope." He sat up and smiled. He looked rested for the first time, and his color had returned. He lighted a cigarette. "Nope, I didn't break. Close, though," he said, his blue eyes twinkling, and he held his thumb and index finger a pencil width apart. "Close."

I grinned, as if his triumph were my own. "You really got through it, huh? What'd you do? Where were you all night?"

"Right here. While you were working, I was sleeping like a baby. I got back here late, from the AA meeting. I just told 'em I was sick, they could dock my pay, and then I came back and slept the night away."

"Wow! That's great!" I shook his hand. "See, man, that's what I've been telling you! You got to keep going to those AA meetings."

He smiled tolerantly, rubbed out his cigarette and lay back down. I pulled off my shirt and trousers, climbed up to my bed, and when I heard Bob snoring, fell asleep.

That afternoon, when I woke, Bob was gone again. I got down from my bed and noticed that his cardboard suitcase was gone too. His drawer in the dresser was empty, and when I looked into the medicine cabinet above the tiny sink in the corner, I saw that he'd taken his shaving kit. He'd moved out.

I was confused and suddenly, unexpectedly, sad. I stood in front of the mirror and shaved, the first time in three days, and tried to figure it all out—Bob's alcoholism, which did indeed seem as much a part of him as his height or the color of his eyes, and my caring about it; his persistent advice to me, and mine to him; his vain dream of not drinking, my dream of . . . what? Success? Forgiveness? Revenge? Somehow, Bob and I were alike, I thought, especially now that he had fled from the hotel. The thought scared me. It was the first time since that snowy night I left the college on the hill that I'd been scared.

I wiped off the scraps of shaving cream, washed my razor, and opened the cabinet for my Aqua Velva. Gone. Bob must have taken it, I thought. A wave of anger swirled around me and passed quickly on. I sighed. Oh, what the hell, let him have it. The man left without even one week's pay; a morning splash of aftershave would make him feel successful for at least a minute or two. The rest of the day he'll feel like what he is, I thought, a failure.

I picked up my shirt and pants and slowly got dressed, when, leaning down to tie my shoe, I saw the pale blue bottle in the tin trash can between the dresser and the bed. I reached in, drew it out and saw that it was empty. I knew at once that Bob had drunk it down.

Chucking it back, as if it were a dead animal, I looked around the gray room, and I saw its pathetic poverty for the first time—the spindly furniture, the bare cinder-block walls and linoleum floor, the small window that faced the yellow-brick side of the parking garage next door. Heinz's blue Buick was probably still parked there. I looked at my half-dozen paperback books on the dresser—mysteries, a Stendhal novel, an anthology of *Great American Short Stories*—and my papers, a short stack of letters from home, a sketchbook, a journal I was planning to write in soon. I'd bought it for Cuba. Then I pulled my old canvas duffel out from under the bed and began shoving clothes inside.

I rented a room from an old lady who owned a small house off Central Avenue in downtown St. Petersburg, a quiet neighborhood of bungalows and tree-lined streets that was beginning to be devoured at the edges by glass-and-concrete buildings that housed condominiums, insurance companies and bank branches. The room was small but bright and clean, in the back off the kitchen, with its own bathroom and separate entrance. With the room went kitchen privileges, but I would have to eat in my bedroom. There were strict house rules that I eagerly agreed to: no visitors, by which I knew she meant women; no smoking; no drinking. I'd been meaning to give up smoking anyhow, and since the only way I could drink was more or less illegally, it seemed more or less a luxury to me. Especially after Bob O'Neil. As for women in my room, based on my experience so far, the old lady might as well have said no Martians.

"I'm a Christian," she said, "and this is a Christian home." Her name was Mrs. Treworgy. She was tiny, half my size, and pink—pink hair, pink skin, pink rims around her watery eyes.

"I'm a Christian too," I assured her.

"What church?"

I hesitated. "Methodist?"

She smiled, relieved, and told me where the nearest
Methodist church was located; not far, as it turned out. She
herself was a Baptist, which meant that she had to walk ten
blocks each way on Sundays. "But the preaching's worth it,"
she said. "And our choir is much better than the Methodists'."

"I'm sure."

"Maybe you'd like to come with me some Sunday."

"Oh, yes, indeed I would," I said. "But I'll probably try
the Methodist church first. You know, since it's what I'm
used to and all." What I was used to was sleeping till noon
on Sundays and before that, when my mother made me go,
dozing through mass.

"Yes, of course." Then she asked for the first and last
months' rent in advance. Eighty dollars.

"I only have sixty-seven dollars to my name," I said. I confessed as if to a crime that I had just quit my job at the Coquina Key Hotel and briefly described the conditions there,
as if they were extenuating circumstances. "It was a very
. . . unsavory atmosphere," I said, looking at the floor of her
living room. The room was small, crowded with large, dark
furniture and portraits of Jesus, close-ups and long shots,
seated by a rock at prayer and ascending like Superman into
heaven.

She looked at me carefully. "You have an honest face,"
she pronounced. "I'm sure you'll find a new job right away.
Whyn't you just pay me the first month's rent, forty dollars,
and we'll go from there."

"Oh, thank you, Mrs. Treworgy. Thank you. And you
wait," I said. "I'll have a job by tomorrow!"

Which I did. Following at last the advice of my ex-
roommate Bob O'Neil, I applied for a job where I could be
seen, as a menswear salesman at the fashionable downtown
Maas Brothers Department Store. On the application form,
however, under hobbies, I wrote "drawing and painting"

and was instead hired to work in the display department as an assistant window trimmer. The display department was located in the basement of the large, modern building, and as an assistant I was expected to build and paint the backdrops for the interior and window displays designed and installed by a tall, thin, Georgia man named, appropriately, Art, and a bulky, middle-aged, black-haired woman named Sukey, who wore turquoise and silver Indian jewelry and hand-printed muumuus. Art was an agreeable man in his forties who'd been in advertising in Atlanta until a decade ago, when his ulcers erupted and sent him to the hospital for the third time in one year, after which he'd quit and moved to Florida. He popped antacid tablets all day, and his mouth was perpetually dry and white-lipped, but he joked and smiled easily, teased Sukey for her artistic pretensions, me for my youth and ignorance and Ray, the obese, bald sign-painter, for his weight and baldness.

It was a cheerful, easygoing place, especially after the Coquina Key Hotel, and I enjoyed the work, which was not difficult. I built lightweight wood frames, usually four feet by eight feet, covered them with colored paper or foil, painted screens and backdrops, cleaned brushes and swept the floor of the shop. Afternoons, I delivered signs for Ray to the department heads upstairs, ate lunch with the salespeople and the rest of the staff in the company cafeteria on the first floor, and after work, went out for beers with Art, Sukey and Ray and then walked whistling back to my room at Mrs. Treworgy's, where, after supper, I drew pictures, usually somber self-portraits, read and prepared to write in my journal.

I turned nineteen that spring, and there were pink, white and yellow hibiscus blossoms everywhere and sweet-smelling jasmine, oleander and poinciana trees in bloom. Palm trees fluttered in the warm breezes off the Gulf, and tamarind trees clacked their long dark pods, while citrus trees in backyards produced huge, juicy oranges for the plucking. I wore short-sleeved shirts, light cotton trousers, sandals, and felt my body gradually cease cringing from the remembered New England cold and begin to expand and move out to meet this new world. I was tanned and well fed, muscular and extremely healthy, and my mind, naturally, began turning obsessively to thoughts of women.

Even though it was only a respite, for the first time since the previous December I felt free of guilt for failing at life before trying first to succeed, and freed from such a complex, burdensome guilt, I was trapped instantly by lust. Not ordinary lust, but late-adolescent, New England virginal lust, lust engendered by chemistry crossed with curiosity, lust with no memory to restrain and train it, lust that seeks not merely to satisfy and deplete itself, but to avenge itself as well. For the first time in my life, I seemed to be happy and consequently wanted only to make up for lost time and lost opportunities, to get even with all those Catholic schoolgirls who'd said, "Stop," and I stopped, all those passionate plunges frozen in agonizing positions in midair over car seats, sofas, daybeds, carpeted living room floors, beach blankets and hammocks, all those semen-stained throw pillows on the asbestos tile floors of pine-paneled basement dens. This was lust with a vengeance.

The male of the species ceased to exist. Walking to work in the morning, I saw only women and girls getting on and off buses, stepping from parked cars, long brown legs drawing skirts tightly against tender thighs, blouses whose sole function seemed to be to draw my attention to breasts. At lunch in the cafeteria, I looked watery-eyed and swollen across the food counter at the black women, the first I'd seen up close, all shades of brown and black, from pale gold and coffee to maple red and mahogany, their dark eyes looking straight through me, as if I were invisible, and when I tried to smile, to be seen, and now and then succeeded, I quickly dropped my eyes and moved down the line to the cash regis-

ter, where, as I paid, I searched the cafeteria for the girl
who'd been standing next to me in line, a salesgirl I'd once
heard talking to Sukey in the basement shop about eye
makeup and had watched from then on every chance I got,
always from a safe distance, however, as she had strawberry
blond, wavy, shoulder-length hair that made my hands open
and close involuntarily, large green eyes that made my lips
dry out, a soft Southern accent that made my breath come
in tiny packets.

It was as if my awareness of my surroundings were determined by a glandular condition. After work, I sat with Art,
Sukey and Ray in the bar on the corner across from the store,
and while they spoke to one another and to me, I watched
the girls from the store like a panther about to pounce,
watched them smoke their cigarettes and talk, slender wrists
flicking, gold bracelets catching light and bouncing it
through smoke off the walls, moist red lips nipping at the air,
parting for white teeth, pink wet tongues, little cries of
laughter. I began to wonder what Sukey looked like under
her throat-to-ground muumuu and imagined hot loaves of
flesh. Delivering signs for Ray to swimwear on the second
floor, I rode the escalator up from the first and sniffed the
air eagerly and caught the scent of perfume, lipstick, shaved
underarms, and nearly tripped at the top. I went to church
with Mrs. Treworgy, got lost watching the teenaged girls in
the choir, and as we left I inadvertently crossed myself,
which I knew Protestants did not do, though I told Mrs. Treworgy that we Methodists sometimes did. I was invited by
Art to have dinner with him and his wife, and throughout
the meal wondered how Art would take it if I had a brief
love affair with his dark, bouffant-haired wife, who asked me
if people from New England really did say, "Pahk the cah
in Hahvahd Yahd," and if so, why didn't I talk that way? I
told her they did and I did, and for the rest of the evening
I did.

To save myself from abject humiliation and worse, I did

what men usually do in this situation. I went back to guilt
and became obsessed with my work. I decided to succeed
in this new trade, to become the best assistant window trimmer that had ever worked at Maas Brothers. It was time, I
decided, for me to make my move. I drew window displays
in my room at night, anything to keep my mind and hands
busy at the same time. Some of the designs were for windows
that exhibited spring dresses, but more often they portrayed
less agitating merchandise, like air conditioners, men's
shoes, lawn mowers and lamps. Many of them were inven-
tive and well-drawn designs that the next day I left lying
around Art's workbench and Sukey's easel, even leaving my
pad open next to Ray's brushes when I went upstairs for his
midmorning snack. I figured that once I was permitted to
design and install my own window, my talent would be recognized and I'd be promoted, on my way. With a new kid
hired to replace me as assistant, Art or Sukey would be
moved to the larger store in Tampa or shifted to the Maas
Brothers about to open in Miami. I'd follow a few years later,
only to pass them by, moving swiftly up the ladder of window trimming to where the only moves left to me would be
horizontal, into management, vice-president in charge of advertising, and on up from there.

Then it happened. One morning in May, I came whistling
cheerfully into the shop, as was my habit, and Art called me
aside and said that there was going to be a fashion show in
swimwear that afternoon and they needed a tropical-island
floor display right away. "Sukey and me are all tied up getting them damned Memorial Day windows done," he
drawled. "Whyn't you all try your hand on the tropical island?"

"Why, sure," I said. I flipped open my sketchbook.
"What've you got in mind, Art? I'll work up some sketches."

"Oh, nothing much. They ain't expecting much. Just
some kind of backdrop, some grass or sand, a mannequin in
a swimsuit and maybe a coupla colored spots. You can do it.

I seen your drawings lying around. Now's your opportunity to show us what you can do on your own." He smiled down at me and winked.

I made my sketches, a four-by-eight-foot panel with broad streaks of rose, silver, and orange to signify a tropical sunset, three or four long palm fronds on the upper left corner of the panel and two women, one standing, looking mournfully out to sea, her hands at her eyes, as if watching in vain for her lover's return, the other seated, contemplating the pink and white gauze blossoms that I planned to scatter over the earth.

Then I went to work. I cut two-by-fours for the frame, instead of the usual one-by-twos, nailed them together with eightpenny nails, cross-braced it horizontally and vertically, cut and nailed on plywood triangles to square the corners, and covered both sides with tautly drawn metallic paper, stapling back and hiding the seams neatly, so that, finished, it resembled nothing so much as a solid block of sea-blue steel. They'll use this panel for years, I gloated, and indeed, when I stood the panel up, it was like a well-made house, an oak tree, a piece of public sculpture that would outlive the culture that produced it.

The others went up to lunch, but I stayed down in the shop painting streaks of cloud and sunlight on my panel. "Don't fuss with that thing too long now," Art called back. "You got to have that display done and in by two. The fashion show starts up at two."

"No sweat!" I hollered. I had everything I needed out and arranged neatly before me: the two mannequins, wigs, one blond, one brunette, gauze blossoms, palm fronds, colored spots and extension cords, and the tools I'd need to set them up—hammer, screwdriver, screws and angle iron to fasten the panel to the island, tape, stapler and so on. All I needed now was the bathing suits.

I telephoned swimwear from Art's office. One of the salesgirls answered, and instantly, though she said nothing more than "Swimwear," I recognized the voice. Two notes, and I knew the entire tune. It was the girl I'd overheard talking to Sukey about eye makeup, the strawberry blond I'd studied from a distance in the cafeteria, the green-eyed beauty in the crowd at whom I'd aimed my hunter's gaze from the corner booth after work.

I cleared my throat and stammered that I needed a pair of bathing suits for the fashion show display.

"Okay," she sang. "We're trying on bathing suits right now, for the show and all, so whyn't you come on up and just pick out what you all want?"

"Sure, fine. Sure, that's great, a great idea. Ah . . . who'll I ask for? What's your name?"

"Eleanor," she said, the word rising in my mind like an elegant seabird against a silver moon over dark Caribbean waters.

"Sure. Fine. Eleanor, then. Okay, then . . ."

"G'bye," her voice chimed in my ear.

I put down the phone and decided to take my panel to the second floor right away, to set it up first and then see which bathing suits matched the colors of my sunset before I made my selection. It was surprisingly heavy. In fact, I could barely lift it. I tipped it, got leverage, lifted and carried the panel out of the shop, ducking at the door to keep it from scraping, and managed to get it all the way up the wide stairs from the basement to the first floor before I had to stop and rest a minute. The store was jammed with lunch-hour shoppers, women mostly, many of whom gazed with what I took to be admiration at my blue panel, which by now I regarded as very nearly a work of art.

The escalators were located at the center of the large, crowded floor, where the ceiling swooped and opened up to reveal the second floor as a kind of mezzanine. I could see young women strolling about in bathing suits up there, bare shoulders, naked arms and legs, bare feet, pink arches, toes.

I hefted my panel, got it balanced and moved carefully

through the throng of shoppers to the escalator and got in line. By the time I stepped onto the metal stairs, the panel had grown heavy again, so I set it down, placing one corner on the step. I peered around it and up and caught a glimpse of the girl named Eleanor, wearing a two-piece bathing suit, blood red it was, and very revealing, for in that instant I saw that she had large, high breasts and a navel, my God, a female navel—when I noticed something falling lightly past my face, like sprinkles of dust. Then I heard a loud grinding noise from overhead, screams from below, and debris started falling all about me. I looked up and saw that the top edge of my panel was digging a trench into the ceiling, a gouge that ripped away plaster, wires, pipes, and tubes, and the higher we rode on the escalator, my panel and I, the deeper into the ceiling it dug, relentlessly, as if with rage, while women above and below me, pushing and grabbing one another in fear, shrieked and ran to escape falling chunks of ceiling.

I let go of the panel, but it held there, rigid, like a plowblade, jammed now between the metal tread of the escalator and the ceiling above, which curved lower and lower as we neared the second floor, until the ceiling was almost low enough for me to reach up and touch, when the top of the panel ground itself against the reinforced-concrete floor of the mezzanine itself, and promptly the metal stair began to give. The panel, however, refused to give. It creaked, bowed a little, but it held. The escalator kept on moving, while the noise level rose—screams, shouts, cries for help, falling debris, wood grinding against concrete, metal bending under wood—until at last the ceiling curved up and away from the stairwell, and my panel sprung free, rising like a mainsail, floating over the rail and then tumbling onto the adjacent down escalator, where people ran in horror as it bounced heavily end over end toward glass counters filled with cosmetics, notions, jewelry, perfumes.

Up above, still riding the escalator, I watched with almost

scientific detachment as the stair, bent by the panel into a
shallow V, neared the slot in the floor where the stairs in
front of it one by one flattened neatly and slid away. I saw
the bent stair hit the slot, felt the whole escalator beneath
my feet buckle and jump, heard the motor grind on stub-
bornly, until at last it stopped.

All the electricity in the building had gone off. We were
in a dusky haze, as if after a terrorist's attack. It was silent,
with smoke and dust hovering in the air. A chunk of rubble
rolled into a corner. Water splashed aimlessly from a broken
pipe. A fluorescent light fixture held by a single wire broke
loose and fell to the floor. A woman sobbed. A mother called
her child.

I was at the top of the stairs, facing swimwear. Before me
stood several girls in bathing suits, their hands fisted in horror before open mouths, their eyes wild with fear. One or
two wept quietly. I saw the girl named Eleanor among them,
and I turned and ran blindly back down the way I had just
ridden to the top, leaping over rubble and shoving my way
past terrified shoppers, stunned men in business suits, jani-
tors, salesgirls, crunching over broken glass toward the door
and away from the crowd that had emerged from the cafeteria, past a white-faced Art and Sukey, and out, finally, to the
street. My chest heaved furiously, my ears rang, and still I
ran, charging through traffic without looking, as fire trucks
and police cars with sirens wailing pulled up at the store.

I was in a small park, walking slower and slower along
a white crushed-stone pathway that curved around flower-
beds. There were live oak trees overhead with Spanish moss
hanging down, and small birds flitted in and out of the pale
green leaves. Finally, I stopped. For the first time since that
snowy night in December, I stopped. I sat down on a bench
and put my head in my hands. I believed that my life had
all but ended. I was wrapped entirely in shame, as if in a
shroud. It was a new feeling, a horrible one, for it surrounded
me, enveloping my mind and body totally. There was no way

out of it. In those few moments in the park in St. Petersburg, immolated by endless shame, I was every man who had failed, who had run out on job, family, children, friends— who had run out on *opportunity.* I was Bob O'Neil drunk and lying about it in Florida, my father silent and withdrawn in northern New Hampshire, and me, the boy who went up the hill and then, inexplicably, turned around and came back down empty-handed. I was Little Boy Blue asleep with his horn while the sheep roamed the meadow and the cows ate the corn. I was ashamed for all of us, every one.

Then, gradually, I felt the presence of a hand on my shoulder. I sat up and turned, followed the delicate white hand on my shoulder out to a woman's arm. It was Eleanor, and her green eyes were filled with pity, endless pity that matched my endless shame. She was wearing the dark red bathing suit that I had loved, and she reached forward and placed her naked arms around my chest and laid her head on my shoulder. I smelled her hair, felt her smooth skin against mine.

We stayed like that for a long time, I on the bench, she standing behind me, both of us weeping silently, me in shame and she in pity, until it was almost dark. And that is how I met my first wife, and why I married her.

The Gully

The young man called Freckle Face, whose true name was Naldo de Arauja, was a bus driver with a dangerous route— through the Gully and along the waterfront to the airport and back, turning around at Central Square, where all the buses turn around, and doing it again, four times a day. He was only twenty years old, unmarried and making good money as a driver, and despite his many freckles and reddish hair, he was attractive to the women, possibly because he had lots of money to spend on taking them dancing, buying them Johnnie Walker Red and giving them little presents, such as nylons and stuffed animals. He lived for the women, as he himself often said, and when he was robbed in his bus in the Gully in the middle of the day twice in one week, he was angry enough to kill someone for it, especially after the cops laughed at him and the dispatcher at the bus depot told him that if he got robbed one more time this month he would be fired.

"It's company policy, Freckle Face," he said. "Three times in a month, and you're gone, man." The dispatcher stood in the garage holding his clipboard, waiting for the keys to the bus.

"Why?" Freckle Face asked. "What the hell good does it do to fire the driver? Tell me that."

"Sometimes the drivers are in cahoots with the thieves. Not that you'd do such a thing, but even so, the company's got to have a policy. You know how it is."

Freckle Face handed over the keys, stalked out of the garage, and went straight to a gambler he knew in the Gully two blocks from where he lived and bought a dark blue .45 and box of bullets. He put the loaded gun inside his lunch bag, and when a few days later he stopped at the corner of Angelina and Fourteenth and picked up two men wearing rumpled tan safari jackets to cover the pistols stuck in their belts, Freckle Face simply waited until they had paid and sat down, one of them in the rear and the other directly behind him, as usual with thieves, and he reached down to his lunch bag on the floor, drew out the .45, spun around and shot the man behind him in the eye.

The other man leapt out the back door to the street and started running. Freckle Face grabbed the first one's pistol from where it had fallen to the floor, stepped over the man's body and jumped to the street, like Gary Cooper or Clint Eastwood, a gun in each hand. People in the bus and on the street and sidewalks, mostly women and children at this time of day, were terrified, a few were screaming, but when Freckle Face took off down the street after the second thief, everyone stepped back and cheered.

He caught the guy in a dead-end alley behind a Pakistani restaurant, and he shot him twice, first in the chest and then up close, in the head. He took his gun, too, and walked quickly back to the bus, which was still sitting at the corner of Angelina and Fourteenth with the doors open and the motor running. He climbed into the bus, dragged the body of the first thief out to the street, put all three guns into his lunch bag and continued down Angelina and on out to the airport.

He himself never mentioned the event to anyone, but in

a short time everyone knew about it—the dispatcher, the other drivers, the people and merchants in the Gully and the thieves. People started waiting especially for Freckle Face's bus, letting earlier buses go past. He was extremely popular with the women on his route, who smiled and hitched their dresses up their thighs a little as they climbed the steps of his bus and dropped their coins slowly, one by one, into his hand. No one, of course, mentioned to Freckle Face that they knew what he carried inside his lunch bag, and no one said anything to the police about it. When the police drove into the Gully to pick up the bodies of the two thieves, everyone on the street denied knowing how the men had died. "Who knows?" they shrugged. "Somebody just dumped the bodies there during the night or maybe this morning, when no one was looking. It happens all the time around here. You know that."

Over on the north side of the Gully, not far from the bus depot, a young man called Chink, whose real name was Felipe da Silva, worked in his parents' bakery with his mother, father and two younger sisters. One morning when he came into work late and hung over and expecting the usual harangue from his father, he met instead with the aftermath of a massacre. Moments before, robbers had walked into the shop and killed with guns and machetes all four members of Chink's family plus two customers, elderly ladies from the neighborhood. The white walls, floors, even the ceiling, were splattered with blood, grisly maps showing where the people had met their deaths and how. Chink's sisters had been shot in the front room of the shop, where they worked behind the counter, and the two old neighborhood ladies had been killed, each of them shot once behind the ear, just inside the door. They had probably walked in on the robbery. Chink's father had been cut down with a machete at the doorway leading from the back room, where the ovens were located, and his mother, also chopped practically in half by the machete, had been slain near the back door, evidently fleeing from the carnage.

Chink paused before each body, examined it for a second, stepped over it to the next, careful not to step into the huge spreading smears of thickening blood and flour, until he worked his way to the back, where he found his mother's body. Opening the door to the alley in back, he stepped out, and when he knelt down to the ground, as if to pray or vomit, he saw several pairs of white footprints that led down the alley toward the rear of the building.

Instantly, Chink set off in pursuit of whoever had laid down the tracks. He jogged down the alley, turned left behind the building and climbed over a ramshackle wood fence to another alley, passed through to a packed dirt yard shared by the backsides of a half-dozen tin-roof shanties, where he followed the white footprints across the yard to the rear of an old dark green panel truck sitting wheelless up on cinderblocks. He tiptoed to the rear door of the truck and listened and heard the men inside counting the few miserable dollars they had taken from the bakery. First, he dropped an old piece of iron pipe into the latch, jamming it. Then he walked out to the street to a filling station, boldly stole a five-gallon can of gasoline and brought it back to the panel truck, where he splashed the gasoline onto the packed dirt ground all around the truck, especially at the rear entrance, and poured more gas over the top and along the sides. Last, he lit a match, tossed it at the truck and ran.

People had watched the entire process from the beginning, and no one said or did a thing to stop Chink, and when the truck exploded in a fireball, the folks in the shanties, many of them mothers with babies on their hips, shouted with obvious pleasure. Later, when the firemen had put out the flames and opened the rear door of the truck, three charred, utterly unrecognizable bodies were discovered huddled inside. No one from the shanties knew who they were, how they got locked inside the truck or who doused the truck with gasoline and set it on fire. "We were inside cooking food," they said. And no one—that is, no one from the police or fire department—connected the bizarre incineration of the three young men in the panel truck to the massacre of the six people in the bakery two blocks away. In the Gully, however, everyone knew of the connection and spoke of Chink with sympathy and admiration, even those who used to think of him as a lazy, drunken playboy supported by his industrious family.

Then there was Saverio Gómez Macedo, called Tarzan, because of his great size and overdeveloped physique and the special way he cupped his hands around his mouth and yelled, which he liked to do at the start of every day. He would untangle himself from his hammock on the porch of his grandmother's shanty, step to the standpipe by the alley, where the people were already lining up to fill their pans and jars with water for cooking, and he'd give his yell and beat good-naturedly on his enormous chest.

In exchange for caring for his aged grandmother, who was crippled with arthritis, Tarzan was allowed to sleep on the porch of her cabin. Now and then he got himself hired for daywork, hauling bricks or laying sewer pipe down by the waterfront where the government was building hotels for foreigners, but most of the time he had no money and depended on his grandmother for everything. She, in turn, depended on her children, Tarzan's aunts and uncles, several of whom now lived in Florida and sometimes sent money.

The daughter who was Tarzan's mother had died of cancer many years before, and no one knew who his father was. Thus Tarzan and his grandmother were as close as mother and son. They spent most of their days and evenings sitting out on the shaded, tilted porch of the tiny cabin, where they watched the people pass on the street and chatted and gossiped about the old days and people they used to know. Despite his great size and obvious high spirits, Tarzan was in many ways like a little old man, which, of course, delighted his grandmother and amused everyone in the neighborhood who knew them.

For that reason most people were amazed by the transformation that Tarzan went through when his grandmother was killed. Her death was an unfortunate accident, and perhaps they expected him simply to accept it as such, as they certainly would have, but he treated it as if it were a cold-blooded murder. Two drug dealers in the neighborhood got into a scuffle over money, not an unusual event, and while chasing each other down the alleys and across the yards of the neighborhood, shooting whenever they caught sight of each other, one of them (it was never determined which one) shot Tarzan's grandmother, who was sitting on the porch waiting for Tarzan to come home from the store. She died instantly, shot in the throat, just as Tarzan rounded the corner and saw the pair of drug dealers dart between cars on the street, still shouting at one another, heading out of the neighborhood into another. He roared, pounded his chest in rage, frightening those who heard him, and took off after the drug dealers.

He caught up with them late that night in the back room of a bar out near the airport. Apparently they had settled their differences and were once again doing business with one another, when Tarzan, huge with his anger and his fearlessness, walked into the dingy room, grabbed the two scrawny punks and dragged them out to the street. It was raining, and the street was quiet and almost empty. The bartender and the few customers who were there at the time later described with a kind of horror, a horror oddly mixed with pride, the sound of the skulls cracking as the enormous young man slammed the two men's heads against one another. Then, when clearly they were dead in his hands, Tarzan tossed the pair like sacks of garbage into the gutter and walked off in the rain. After that, because for a while the drug dealers stayed away, but also because of his pain, Tarzan was a hero in the neighborhood.

In the Gully, true heroes were almost nonexistent. Politicians and soldiers had lived off the people for generations, and athletes, singers, actors—figures whose famous faces were used to sell things people either did not otherwise want or could not afford—were, because of that, no longer trusted or admired or even envied. In the Gully, people had grown cynical. It was their only defense against being used over and over to fatten the already fat. They had learned long ago that it's the poor who feed the rich, not vice versa. And finally, when it was almost too late and they had almost nothing left to give to the rich, to the politicians, to the businessmen, to the foreigners, finally the people of the Gully had turned away from all projects and enterprises, all plans, all endeavors that depended for their completion on hope. And when you give up hope, and do it on principle—that is, when you do it because you have learned that hope is *bad* for you— then you give up on heroes as well.

That is why, when Freckle Face heard people praise Chink and then Tarzan and saw how people admired them for their pain and their rage, when, in short, he realized that he and the other two had become heroes, where before there were none, he determined to capitalize on it as swiftly as possible, before people settled back into their old ways of dismissing heroism as a trick.

He organized a meeting of the three in the back room of a café close to his rooming house, and when they had shaken hands, each of them slightly in awe of the other two, for they were as unused to genuine heroes as everyone else in the Gully, Freckle Face got quickly down to business. His plan was to build a watchtower in the center of the Gully and for one of them to be posted there at all times, and when he saw a robbery going on, to give the signal, and the others would chase down the robbers and kill them.

"What for?" Chink asked.

"For money," Freckle Face said.

"Who'd pay us?" Tarzan wanted to know.

"The robbers' victims," Freckle Face explained. "We just return what was stolen and ask for a percentage for our troubles."

"It's wrong to kill for money," Tarzan said.

"God kills. You just pull the trigger," Chink observed. He was definitely interested. Since the death of his parents and sisters, the bakery had been closed, and Chink was down to panhandling on Central Square with a sign around his neck that said, "Help the Avenger of the Bakery Massacre!"

Tarzan needed money, too. With his grandmother's death, his uncles and aunts had sold her shanty to a man on the Heights who rented out hundreds of shanties in the Gully. Consequently, Tarzan had lately been sleeping under two sheets of corrugated iron in back of a warehouse where he hoped to find work as a warehouseman, as soon as his aunt in Florida sent him the money he needed to bribe the foreman to hire him.

Freckle Face was not much better off. His popularity as a bus driver had cut into the income of the other drivers, and in recent weeks Freckle Face had come into work and found sugar in his gas tank one day, his tires slashed another, or a radiator hose cut, a distributor cap missing, every day another lengthy repair job that kept him in the garage, until he was taking home less than half of what he had been earning before the robberies. He'd stopped buying presents for his girlfriends, and they in turn had stopped turning down other guys. He used to be able to get several women to share him; now, despite being a hero, he could barely get one woman to wait for him to get off work and take her out dancing. A hero without money is just another man.

In short order, Freckle Face, Chink and Tarzan were making more money than they had ever imagined possible. Quickly they had specialized, Tarzan as lookout, because of his ability to call out the location and route of a thief spotted from the watchtower. He owned a voice so large and clear that every time he gave the alarm, the entire neighborhood became instantly involved in the pursuit and capture of the chief. Often, all Chink and Freckle Face had to do was follow along the pathway in the street that the crowd opened up for them and run directly down the alley people pointed at, enter the basement door indicated by an old woman with her chin, cross into the corner of the basement that stood exposed by a watchman with a flashlight, where Chink would take out the gun Freckle Face had given him and fire two bullets neatly into the man's head. That was Chink's specialty, shooting, and he did seem to believe that God did the killing, he only did the shooting.

Freckle Face's specialty might be called brokerage. It was he who unclamped the dead thief's fingers from the stolen money and delivered it back to the shopowner or pedestrian who'd been robbed, and he, therefore, who negotiated the price of the return, he who divided the fee three ways. Also, when it became clear that, if they wished, they could expand their business to other neighborhoods in the Gully, it was Freckle Face who arranged to have the new lookout towers built, he who hired the new lookouts, shooters and collectors and he who knew to put Tarzan in charge of all the lookouts and train them to cup their hands just so and call out exactly, clearly, as loud as a siren, where the thieves were running to. It was Freckle Face who put Chink in charge of procuring weapons for the shooters and training them to use their guns efficiently and responsibly, and of course it was he who trained the collectors, implemented the commission system based on the system used by the bus company and kept track of all the accounts.

By now, Tarzan owned his own house on the Heights, where he liked to throw wild, lavish parties by the pool, and Chink lived in a condominium on the waterfront, where he kept a forty-foot cabin cruiser anchored year round, and Freckle Face was sleeping with the daughter of the prime minister. They had come a long ways from the Gully and did not believe that they would ever have to return, especially Freckle Face, who had made a whole new set of friends who called him Naldo and barely knew where in the city the Gully was located.

Sometimes, though, late at night, Freckle Face would rise up from the bed he shared with the daughter of the prime minister, and he'd cross the parquet floor to the louvered doors that led to the terrace, and out on the terrace in the silvery moonlight, he'd lean over the balustrade, light a cigarette and look down and across the sleeping city all the way to the Gully. He'd stand there till dawn, smoking and waiting for the sun to come up and for the people down in the Gully to come out of their shanties and go for water, start up their cook fires, head down to the waterfront looking for work or out to the airport to panhandle tourists or over to Central Square just to hang out in the shade of the mimosa trees. Freckle Face, miles away, up on his terrace, wearing a blue silk robe and smoking French cigarettes, would say over and over to himself, as if it were a magical charm, an incantation: I don't live there anymore, and no one I know lives there. The people who go on living there must want to live there, or they'd leave that place. Look at Tarzan, look at Chink, look at me!

Then he'd go inside, shower, shave and dress, and walk downstairs for breakfast, where the first thing he'd do was read the morning newspaper for the names and addresses of thieves shot by his men last night in the Gully. After breakfast, he'd drive out in his brown Mercedes and call on the families of the dead thieves, offering first his condolences and then his card and a special cut-rate coffin and burial service from his Our Lady of the Gully Funeral Parlor chain. Later on, he'd drop by the office and go over the figures. After that, lunch. Then a workout and a massage. Then— who knows? Real estate, maybe. Import-export. Hotels. Life is certainly surprising, he'd think.

Adultery

———•————⊂✄

By the time I was nineteen years old I had broken all but three of the Ten Commandments. I'd made no graven image, had killed no one and had not committed adultery. On the other hand, I lied, did not keep the Sabbath holy, did not honor my mother and father, especially my father, and I stole—not much, but enough to count as a violation. I'd done it as recently as last week, skimming a few bucks from the night's take at the Thom McAn's out at the Pinellas Shopping Mall, where I worked nights. Selling shoes was a second job—I was saving a thousand dollars for my forthcoming marriage to Eleanor Hastings, an event I'd begun to imagine as capable somehow of washing me clean, like a baptism.

My marriage was going to be a Fresh Start. The new life would cancel the old life and create a new me, a youth who no longer coveted, like the old me, his neighbor's split-level house, his perky, dark wife who looked like Teresa Brewer, new Dodge car, boat, summer vacation, great angular height, Georgia accent. My neighbor was in fact my boss, Art, in the display department at Maas Brothers, where I worked days, a kindly, witty man who now rented the small,

damp basement in his house to me. I coveted everything of
his.

I could see, however, that my neighbor, despite his wit,
was a depressed man, a man who was unhappy being who
he was; thus I wanted to be him and yet somehow still hold
on to the pleasure of being me, too. Perhaps that was the
main attraction of the upcoming marriage. By starting my
life over four months from now, I wouldn't have to give up
my old life; whereas by continuing to covet another man's
life, if I ever actually got what I wanted, I'd lose what I liked.
Such was my morality, then, that I opposed, and preferred,
early marriage to covetousness.

All this anxiety made me feel weak and stupid (which in
turn made me feel something like guilt), but otherwise my
having broken and continuing to break seven of the Ten
Commandments did not especially trouble me. Not deeply.
I'd been unchurched since before my mother stopped making me go to mass, and promises of eternal damnation were
no more able to affect my behavior than were promises of
eternal life. Eternal damnation and life were too hard to picture, like starvation in Africa or Nazi concentration camps,
to make me afraid. This was America in 1959, and most of
us were still dreaming versions of our parents' fading memories—the Depression, War Two, as my father and his friends
called it, and the dying Roosevelt. Instead of fear, I felt incip-
ient guilt.

The idea of breaking the three remaining commandments, however, I treated the way God must have intended
I treat all ten, and I believed that surely, no matter what,
those last three would go unbroken for the rest of my life.
I knew that I would never, under any circumstances, con-
struct a golden calf and fall down before it and offer bloody
sacrifice, acts that seemed somehow sexual and, worse, perverse. And I could not imagine killing another human being.
I'd tried to imagine it, killing was a big part of our childhood
games, but my mind always snapped off, changed reels alto-

gether, just as it came to my turn to kill the Oriental guy charging over the top of Pork Chop Hill swinging a huge Gurkha knife or machete at my throat, bowels, genitals and screaming Chinese Communist obscenities at my Caucasian manhood, mother and homeland. I always dropped my rifle and blacked out and woke up in another movie, a Preston Sturges comedy starring Rex Harrison as conductor of the New York Philharmonic.

As for adultery, my mother some years back, right after the divorce, had broadly hinted that my father had done it. But I never believed her. Not that I thought my father was an especially upright man; he just struck me as sexually unattractive, an ordinary man, like me, and, therefore, not available to women, except to my mother, whom I thought sexually attractive, certainly, but foolish. In my own mildly Oedipal way, I regarded my father as fortunate to have held my mother's sexual interest all those years before the divorce, and his marriage later to a woman who I felt was extremely unattractive proved it.

As for me, when I married, or so I believed, adultery simply could not occur, any more than murder. Though I was a virgin, I was otherwise a healthy adult male, and the idea of making love to one woman whenever I wanted (which was all the time, twenty-four hours a day) was almost too rich a possibility to bear, so that the idea of making love to *more* than one woman was sheer madness, and I avoided thinking it with appropriate diligence.

I was sophisticated enough, however, to know that one could also commit adultery while still single. One could make love to a married woman, for instance, some other man's wife. But this entailed my placing my penis where another man's penis had been, and that, too, seemed a kind of madness or, worse, perverse, like worshiping Jeroboam's golden calf. Perhaps it was our secret reason for wanting virgins for wives: to avoid sexual contact with other men. Regardless, I had never met a married woman to whom I felt sufficiently attracted that I'd risk enraging a husband, a man presumably older than I, since I was only nineteen, which I knew was young to be married, even in Florida. I might indeed covet my neighbor's wife—it was in fact one of the reasons I myself was getting married—but I would not allow myself to be attracted to her.

It was September, hot, sticky, thick with insects the size of bats, and always about to rain or else just drying off from rain, broad leaves dripping and shining in late-afternoon sunlight. We'd scheduled the wedding for January, to let Eleanor turn eighteen—not because we needed to meet the legal requirements (her parents were delighted to see her married, even to someone as young and unaccomplished and adrift as I), but because seventeen seemed too young to *me.* No matter that Eleanor had graduated from high school and was working full time as a salesgirl and bathing suit model in swimwear at Maas Brothers, where in the basement shop I made backdrops for window displays; no matter that for over four years now she'd been physically capable of bearing a child and was as healthy and attractive as a midcentury American female could get; no matter that she loved me deeply, wildly, absolutely, and would never love another; and no matter that I believed I loved her the same way. Somehow, despite all this social, biological and emotional readiness, the mere idea of regular sexual intercourse with a seventeen-year-old girl frightened me. No, I'd wait until she was eighteen; then I'd do it. Marrying and sleeping with a teenager (which, strangely, an eighteen-year-old woman was not) was something rock 'n' rollers like Jerry Lee Lewis and many black people did. Young white working-class males, struggling to move up by dint of hard work, pluck, luck and force of personality, waited.

By waiting, one honored a kind of taboo. One made a virtue of it. It was a way of getting ahead, like taking a corre-

spondence course in accounting or TV repair. One felt virtu-
ous. So that it never occurred to me that I just wanted to get
into bed with Eleanor Hastings, that I wanted only to make
love to her mindlessly for hours, then to fall asleep exhausted
and wake and do it again and then again and not go into
work the next day but stay in bed and sweat and stink and
dry out and sweat some more, to empty myself out, over and
over, for as long as it took to turn me into a husk, and then
shower, dress, smoke a cigarette and move on down the
road, maybe try Miami next, Key West, then the Caribbean.

No, I believed that I wanted a loyal and pretty wife, a lifelong companion, a woman to mother my children, and I
thought that's what Eleanor Hastings wanted too, because
if she didn't, if all that pretty girl wanted was to make love
with me, then, by God, she was not fit to be my wife! And,
naturally, there was no way I would make love to a woman
who was not fit to be my wife. That was *not* how one got
ahead in America. Look at my father, a carpenter in a New
Hampshire mill town living with someone other than my
mother, whom he did not deserve anyhow and therefore did
not have. Life was hard and unequally so, but just.

Then one night late in September I drove my beat-up
gray Studebaker out to the tract house in North St. Petersburg—a barren flatlands then, of shallow swamps, canals and
cheap housing developments—where Eleanor lived with
her parents and two younger sisters and brother. Eleanor's
father installed ceramic tile for a living. He had been seventeen and Eleanor's mother sixteen when Eleanor was born,
which made them thirty-four and thirty-three now—to me,
practically middle-aged. They were Pentecostal Christians,
deep believers. To my relief, Eleanor was not.

Their daughter's apostasy and my having been raised
Catholic didn't trouble them, as it might have worried northern and more liberal Protestants. "The Lord will bring you

to Him in His own time and way, children," her mother declared, beaming. "Meanwhile, we'll pray for you. Won't we, Dad?" she said to her tall, bony, grim husband. He smiled with only his teeth, small and yellow, the rest of his face remaining expressionless, and then they left us alone in the living room.

We were on the couch, side by side, feet planted squarely on the shag-carpeted floor. Eleanor's left hand was wrapped in my right, generating heat, but we got to the subject quickly, because time alone was rare and brief and had to be used efficiently. The sisters were at a church meeting for adolescents, and little brother was confined to his bedroom for having said "You shit!" to his bicycle when it fell over on him in the driveway and scraped his leg.

The subject was Eleanor's virginity, not a subject that I was in the habit of discussing, but all day and now well into the evening my thoughts had been looping toward the subject in an erratic, anxious way, as if it were a persistent back itch just beyond my contorted reach. It may have had to do with the late-summer heat, which reminded me of drive-in movies back home on Route 3 in Hooksett and Bow, New Hampshire, and dozens of high school summertime backseat thrashings, grunts and squirts and the crazed, self-loathing envy born of ignorance and male adolescent brag. Or it simply may have had to do with my growing awareness that I knew as little about Eleanor's past as she did of mine.

"All I know about you," I said, almost a lament, "is what I see and what you've told me."

"That's all anyone knows about anyone, honey. It's all I know about *you*," she said in an accent that Gulf Coast Florida had laid down on her mother's Mississippi drawl, quickening Eleanor's speech without losing the dark, loamy vowels and soft, slurred consonants. My talk was merely that, talk, or so it seemed to me—ideas made over into sounds, feelings translated into symbols and emblems. Hers, though, was the thing itself—food and sunlight and rest. Thus we rarely had actual conversations: I talked, but she spoke, and I heard things, but she listened to them.

"For instance," I said, and cleared my throat, "I know you told me you're still a . . . still a virgin and all, and I believe you, of course. But there's something keeps nagging at me, a sort of intuition or something, and I can't seem to let it go, you know?"

"No, Lovey. What're you tryin' to get to?" I loved it when she called me Lovey. She smiled—large, green, deep-set eyes, long, narrow nose, wide mouth filled with perfect teeth. How could such a goddess love a human boy like me? Unless she was not a virgin.

Of course, I was right: she was not a virgin. She wept, amazed by my powers of perception. "How did you know? How?"

"I just knew you weren't," I told her, a great sadness in my voice. "I don't know how I knew it, but I did, all along. It's in your eyes, somehow, or your mouth. Something. But I couldn't deny it, I knew you weren't a virgin, no matter what you told me, no matter what I wanted to believe. And eventually"—I drawled it out—"eventually I would have found out the truth. It's not a secret a woman can keep forever. Once we were married . . ." I said, and I looked down mournfully at my hands, crossed over one another and open in my lap, as if waiting for a communion wafer.

I felt like a bag of water, but I held myself rigidly in place, kept my voice low and controlled, and when she tearfully asked if this meant that the marriage was off, I assured her that we would still be married, as planned, in January. "Nothing truly important is changed," I said. "I would like to know the details, though."

"Details? What do you mean, Earl?"

"Well, it does make a difference, you know . . . how you lost it, I mean."

"It does?"

"Well . . . yeah, of course."

"I don't understand," she said. "I'm very embarrassed, Earl. The whole thing is just . . . well, it's humiliating! It was so stupid, you know? It wasn't even any fun."

"I suppose if it had been fun, then everything would be okay now."

"No, of course not. Oh, God, I'm so ashamed! Don't make me tell you about it."

"Well, I really do need to know the details. It's important."

"How? Important to what? What possible difference can knowing the details make?"

I took a deep breath. "Well, I need to know, for example, how many times, how often you did it. I guess I need to know a little about the man . . . or men."

"Oh, God, it can't make any difference! Earl, I love you, that's all that counts!" she cried, tears streaming over her cheeks.

"No," I said. "That's not all that counts. There's other things that count too." I examined the palms of my hands.

"Oh." She thought for a moment, then shook her head, and fresh tears sprang from her eyes. "No, I *can't!* I just *can't* tell you! I can barely even admit it to myself!"

I was horrified. I imagined sexual acts so sordid and degrading that, for a brief moment, I forgot about myself and instead felt a flash of sorrow for her. But then, as she managed somehow to face down her memories and told me the story of her first love, a boy she went to high school with and who, on the night of the senior prom, got her drunk on screwdrivers and had his fumbling way with her in the back seat of his dad's car—as she told me this sad, sweet, guilty secret, I felt my sorrow and protectiveness gush from me, leaving me dry and empty and cold, a place where a night wind blew across a desert.

At the end of her confession, I stood. "Well, I have to leave now. It's . . . it's late, and I have to get up early for work."

She looked up at me, her expression a curious mixture of sadness and anger. "It's all over between us now, isn't it?" "No! No, no, it's . . .*changed,*" I said. "But not over. We'll just have to talk some more, I guess. Not now, though. I . . . I have to think things over first," I explained, and I made for the door, before I fell down crying or threw up or broke my hand punching the wall.

She waved from the door as I staggered to my gray car, wrenched open the door, and tossed myself inside. I looked back at the front door of the house, and there they were, Mr. and Mrs. Hastings, standing behind their eldest daughter, waving at me, up and down, sadly, slowly, as if they, too, knew Eleanor's secret, had known it all along and knew now that I had found it out and was in flight, the first of a long line of potential husbands to flee in the night, angry, betrayed, hurt and almost swindled by his own desire.

The problem, of course, lay in the incoherence of my desire. It was too tangled in chains of insecurity, pride, fear, anger and mother love to move responsibly through the lives of decent people. It was desire that was barely conscious of itself; consequently, I was able frequently to deny its existence altogether, which, at such times, made me wonder why I wanted to marry Eleanor in the first place.

I especially wondered it when in the presence of the wife of my neighbor, boss, and landlord, Art Pitman. His wife was small, what we used to call petite, round-faced, with large, dark eyes and a bright, quick smile. Her name was Donna, and when I was in her presence, brushing past her in the hallway as I left for work in the morning, she, in cotton housecoat and fuzzy slippers, retrieving the morning paper from the front steps for Art, who was in the bathroom shaving, I'd catch her smell, a spoor of bed and sweat and sex, and I'd feel myself go weak in the legs, grow cold and then hot, flush red across my face and ears and flood with desire as clear, undeniable and coherent as my desire for Eleanor was muddy, deniable and incoherent. I knew for certain that I wanted to make love to Donna, that and nothing else. I did not want to talk to her, tell her my troubles or secret fears or ambitions, I did not want to brag to her, I did not want to do anything except tear off clothing, draw back the covers of whatever bed was handy and have at it.

Who can say what prompts sexual desire of this sort? Eleanor, by any standard, was more conventionally attractive than Donna, and besides, she was my age, which Donna, in her early thirties, was not. If anything, the quality of my attraction to the two women should have been reversed—neurotic and subterranean for Donna, healthy and straightforward for Eleanor. But we discover ourselves as we can, taking everything that's given us and knowing that it's still only a part of the whole, the tail of the elephant or the trunk or the wide, rounded side. We name the beast as precisely as we can, ass or serpent or whale, name it and move quickly sideways or back, so as not to get kicked by the ass, bit by the serpent, swallowed whole by the whale.

I seem to have spent a great deal of time that year in basements—all day long six days a week in the display shop at Maas Brothers Department Store downtown, and nights, when I was not with Eleanor or at the Pinellas Shopping Mall selling shoes for Thom McAn, in my apartment in the basement of Art Pitman's new split-level house in West St. Petersburg. Real life seemed always to be going on someplace above me, while I toiled, mumbled, listened to the radio, worked, ate, masturbated, read, slept and dreamed below in my damp, dark quarters.

My apartment was a one-room efficiency with access through a common hallway and a first-floor exit, so I could not come and go without letting the Pitmans know, for I rarely came home after midnight, thanks to Eleanor's parents' rules, and I usually left for work in the morning a few minutes before Art. It was the kind of orderly, predictable, serious life that I believed was required of a person who wished to get ahead, and since I so desperately wanted to get ahead, wanted, as it were, to become Art, I did not find that life boring or particularly inhibiting.

Things were coming unraveled, however. I had just discovered that the girl I planned to marry was not a virgin. This did not surprise me, but it hurt and horrified me. I did not know, of course, that my hurt and horror were connected intricately to my abandoned mother in New Hampshire, to my father with his new wife, to the heat I felt in my loins as I lay in my bed in the basement and heard Donna Pitman cross the kitchen floor above me, her high heels clicking against the tile floor.

The loss of Eleanor Hastings's virginity meant that I could no longer idealize her, could not deal with her as an abstraction. It removed her, and therefore me, from ritualized sex, which was the only kind of sex that did not terrify me. But now there was a smoldering in the basement, a bubbling up of adolescent lust, a superheated midden heap of flammable materials wanting only a spark to ignite it. Trouble, terrible trouble, was coming, and I knew it better than anyone.

In my Studebaker that night, I was a madman, foot pressed flat to the floor, swerving from curb to curb as I cut across intersections, downshifting the clumsy, tired car, squealing the tires and racing on, through darkened downtown St. Petersburg and west, past Webb's City and the railroad yards and on out toward the beach and home. My eyes surely bulged, and my teeth probably gnashed, and my fingers clutched the wheel as if trying to strangle it, while my thoughts raved and roared, terror-struck at what now seemed inevitable, enraged at the girl who seemed responsible for having broken the dike, sabotaged the dam, loosed the flood. That *fool!* I thought. How could she have been so stupid! Didn't she realize, that hot, drunken night in May, that she would be responsible a few months later for keeping a wild man under control? Didn't she know that her virginity would be essential to his ability to function rationally in the world? How could she have been so *irresponsible?* It's over, I thought. Oh, boy, is it ever over now. Like Niagara Falls, it's over.

I yanked the wheel to the right and came to a bumpy halt at the curb in front of the house. Art's new green-and-black Dodge was gone from the carport, and the lights in the house were out. I got out my key and stumbled, as if drunk, to the steps and fumbled at the door, when suddenly it opened in as if on its own, and there was Donna, holding open the door for me and wearing, yes, unbelievably, but wearing it nonetheless, what appeared to be no more than a pink dressing gown tied at the throat with a pink ribbon, at the waist with a silken sash, and she was barefoot, I noticed at once, for I looked down as soon as I saw her there, and then I looked up and saw that her short, dark hair was tousled, tossed as if someone's passionate hands had held her head while he stared intently into her pouting, full-lipped face, her eyes half-closed, her nostrils flared, skin drawn tightly back over cheekbones. And, yes, reader, I committed adultery that night. I passed through the door and into the dark hallway, and took the hand of the woman who was married to my boss, a man who had kept me from being fired when everyone at Maas Brothers, it seemed, wanted me fired and had taken me into his home so as to facilitate my entry into adult life, a noble man, an honest man, and compared to me, an innocent man. That man's wife led me to her bed and kept me there for the entire night, until the sun rose, when I, too, rose and then descended to my basement room, where, for about an hour, I pondered the meaning of this event, while I showered, dressed and went whistling off to work.

Throughout that long first night of rising and falling passion, we spoke almost not at all. At first, in the hallway, I asked in a high, windy voice, "Where's Art?" and she said, "Gone to Miami for three days . . . for the store."

"Oh," I said.

A little later, she asked me if this was the first time I'd ever made love to a woman, and I said, "No, not really," and she gave a pleasant little laugh and started kissing me all over my hairless chest again.

When at last I left her bed, she said in a sleepy voice, "Earl, honey, you are the sweetest thing. I got to be careful you don't get to be a habit."

I nodded, as if understanding everything, but I understood nothing. I did *know* certain things, however. I knew, for instance, that in one night Donna had become a habit for me. At least, making love to her had. I still had no interest in becoming her friend, however. What I wanted near me, next to me, around me, was her femaleness, her smooth skin, breasts, nipples, dark thatch of pubic hair, hips, mouth, eyes, ears—I wanted to dive into her as if into a warm, enveloping body of water, to roll, curl and swirl there, floating free of time, fear, greed and dread, never coming up for air to the cold world of men and boys and futures that may or may not turn out well.

Dreams, fantasies, drooling, lascivious wishes, were all amazingly coming true. I rushed straight home from work the next day, and instead of going downstairs to my cellar to change clothes and eat and leave for Thom McAn's, I strolled casually back to the kitchen of Art and Donna's part of the house, and sure enough, there was Donna in a watermelon-pink bikini, smelling of coconut tanning lotion, her hair tied off her slender neck with a black ribbon. She stood at the kitchen counter painting her fingernails to match the bikini, her elbows resting against the Formica, hands like birds touching bills, lovely, small breasts hanging down like soft fruit, plums or tangerines. She turned and cocked her head when I came into the kitchen, smiled, then went quickly back to her nails, while I watched in stunned, admiring silence.

"What you staring at?" she asked without looking up.

I made an uncontrollable noise, "Uh-*huck!*" like Mortimer Snerd, put my hands in my trousers pockets, felt my thighs, and instantly took them out again and started cracking my knuckles like a gangster in a movie about to beat someone to death.

Donna stood back a second, admired her pink fingernails, and suddenly lifted one leg like a dancer and placed the heel of her foot on the counter and began to paint the toenails. I was tumescent. "You want a beer?" she asked. "There's some in the fridge. Get me one, too, will you?"

I grabbed a pair of cans of Colt 45, thrust one at her and wrenched mine open and gulped it down. She turned and watched me, caught me with my eyes filling from the effort of swallowing so much beer so fast and said, "You must be awful thirsty, honey."

"Yeah!"

She smiled benignly and took a ladylike sip from her can. "You got to work at that shoe store t'night?"

"Yeah!" I finished off the beer and crushed the can.

"Too bad," she said, going back to her toenails.

"Yeah! Yeah, it is!"

"You'd probably want to spend the evening out there with your sweetie, anyhow. Whatzername? Eleanor?"

"Yeah, Eleanor. But we . . . had a fight, sort of, so, no . . . no, I wouldn't be going out there tonight, if I didn't have to work. I'd just be hanging around here, prob'ly."

"Keeping me company?" She looked over and winked.

I made that noise again, "Uh-*huck!*" and grinned.

"Well, maybe I'll still be up when you get home," she said, and went back to her nails. "Art's coming home tomorrow," she added, throwing it in as an afterthought.

I swallowed and said nothing.

"You worried about Art?" she asked. "Finding out, I mean."

"*Me?* Hell, no!" I said, my voice rising. "I mean, he'll never find out. Will he?"

She laughed. "Light me a cigarette," she said, pointing

with her chin to a pack of Chesterfield Kings on the table in the breakfast nook. I obeyed and placed the lighted cigarette between her lips, while she worked on her toes with both hands. "No, he'll never find out. You don't have to worry," she said, the cigarette bobbing as she spoke.

From a distance of about a yard, I examined her rounded, barely covered butt, her long, tensed flank, her calf muscle, and longed to run my hands along the length of her extended leg, making it quiver beneath my touch.

"But listen, honey," she said, bringing her foot down and turning to face me, hands on hips. "I got to warn you, Art's got one hell of a crazy temper, so we *both* better hope he never finds out. He may *seem* real quiet and all, but he'd shoot you, and then he'd beat the bejesus out of me."

"How . . . how could he find out?"

"Easy," she said. "If you told someone, down there at the store, say, Maas Brothers, and it got back to Art." She sipped at her beer and regarded me over the top of the can.

"Oh, I'd never do that."

"Okay, but let's say you got to feeling guilty about your sweetie, Eleanor, about being with another woman and all? When you're supposed to be engaged to her? So you get to feeling like you ought to be honest with her and clear the air, you know, like people do sometimes? So you tell her about me and you, and then she gets mad at me for taking her boyfriend, which I'm not doing, of course, but she wouldn't see it that way. So she goes and tells Art, sends him an anonymous letter or phone call, say? It happens, honey. Lots. You wouldn't believe what some women do."

"I'd never tell Eleanor, anyhow!" I said. "Are you kidding? Boy, tell Eleanor. Wow."

"Well, you better not, honey. It's got to be our little secret." She smiled, winked again, and as she eased past me toward the hall, leaned up and kissed me on the lips, quickly, but erotically, a brush, a pink flick of the tongue, and then she was past. "See you tonight?" she asked from the hall.

"Yeah! I . . . I'll be back around ten. Little after."

"That's real good. See you then," she sang, and disappeared around the corner and up the stairs.

I went to the refrigerator and pulled out another can of Art's beer and poured it down my throat. Then I headed downstairs to my basement to change clothes, pummeled, as I descended, by images of Art Pitman, huge, towering with rage, kicking in the door of the bedroom he shares with his wife, flicking on the light, me naked rising on my elbows, as if from the bottom of the sea, Donna rising naked below me, then both of us screaming, as Art pulls out his revolver and starts firing.

Ghastly visions did not keep me from committing adultery, however. Not that night after work at Thom McAn's and not one night a week later, when Art had to attend a convention of department store display directors in Atlanta, and not one Sunday afternoon a few days after that, when Art went fishing in his twenty-foot Boston Whaler with forty-horsepower Evinrude that I coveted. I avoided Eleanor at the store, but several times during that period she called my apartment, and we talked on the telephone, shyly, elusively, briefly. And then one Friday evening we agreed to meet, and the next day after work we met on the street outside the store and walked beneath live oak trees to the park by the library and sat down on the very bench where barely six months before we had pledged undying love to one another.

We observed that things had changed. "Do you still love me, Earl?" she asked, not looking at me. She wore a lemon-yellow blouse with a low, scalloped neckline that revealed her creamy throat in a way that made me catch my breath.

"Yes!" I said. "Yes, I still love you. That's not changed. As a fact, I mean."

"What do you mean?"

"Well, I guess that, while I still love you, I don't believe

I love you in quite the same way, with quite the same . . . innocence."

"It's not you," she said, "who went and lost his innocence."

"Well, yeah, I guess you could say that. But anyhow, I do love you as much as ever. Just . . . differently, that's all." I tried to explain that since there'd been no quantitative change in my love, there'd been no essential qualitative change, either, but she started to cry.

"It's all my fault!" she said.

I put my arms around her and drew her to me. "No, no, Ellie, it's not. And there's nothing truly important that's different now. It's just that I'm a little confused about . . . about what to *do* now. I mean, here I've been holding back, you know, from making love with you, all these months of waiting and being frustrated and waiting some more, thinking it's all worth it because you're still a virgin and all, which is something a man's got to respect, if only because you're always saying, 'No,' and 'That's far enough,' and 'Wait till we're married.' Only now it turns out that there's no real reason to wait till we're married. I mean, with your virginity gone, what's the big deal? It's confusing. All of a sudden it doesn't make sense anymore to wait like we've been doing. Only I still don't feel right about *not* waiting till we're married. Know what I mean?"

"Yes," she said. "You're right." She had stopped crying and was kneading my back with her hands.

"I mean, what the hell? Right?"

"Yes. Right."

"I mean, why keep waiting? Right?"

"Right," she said. "I love you," she murmured into my shirt.

"I mean, why go on dealing with all this frustration?"

"Yes. You're right, Lovey. I agree."

"Yeah. I mean, it seems so . . . dumb. You know?"

"Yes. I agree with you, Earl."

"You do? We'll still get married, of course. That's got nothing to do with this, I mean. Right?"

"Right. Yes."

"Okay, then," I said. "Tomorrow's Sunday. Maybe I'll . . . maybe I'll drive by and pick you up while everyone's at church. Tell them, you tell them, tell them we're going to the beach or something. Okay? And we can come back to my apartment instead."

"Your apartment?"

"Well, yeah. I mean, it's where we can be sure no one will, you know, come in on us or anything. It's what we both want, isn't it?"

"Yes," she said, kneading my back furiously. "I'll make you happy, Lovey. I promise," she said.

"I'll make you happy too," I said.

I didn't drive straight home, as usual, for food and to change shirts; instead, I went out to Thom McAn's early. Having rededicated myself to my plan to save a thousand dollars before Eleanor and I got married, I put in an extra hour, so we could that much more easily set up housekeeping in January in what I regarded as high style, a cinder-block bungalow in a new development by the Gulf—ten percent down, one hundred dollars a month, a carport for my Studebaker, a treeless backyard, sort of a front yard, asbestos tile floors, tiny metal-framed windows already rusting from the sea air.

While I drove and during the four hours at the store when I seemed to be selling shoes, I promised myself that I would never, ever, commit adultery again. I decided to announce this to Donna tonight, if possible, and though she might protest, though she might weep, though she might feel misled, betrayed and rejected by me, I would not relent. I imagined her beating on my chest, a part of my body she seemed particularly attracted to. I would hold her by the wrists, bring them slowly down to her sides, let go and say, "It can't go on any longer. I don't love you, I love Eleanor Hastings and will marry her." Donna, I had come to believe, did not love her husband. She loved me. That's what she had been telling me for several weeks now, over and over in my ear as she writhed beneath me, then in a lilting whisper as I rose from her bed to go, then with a little laugh as I stopped at the door and blew her a kiss. "I surely do love you, Earl," she kept saying. Her husband she referred to only now and then, but always with a sneer, as "that cold fish," implying impotence, and me she referred to frequently as "my little firecracker," implying, I reasoned, the opposite.

In any event, I arrived home from the shoestore fully pre-pared, rehearsed, even, to say goodbye to Donna and adul-tery and consequently was disappointed to see the living room lights on and Art's car parked in the driveway, bright green tail fins reflecting moonlight. I opened the front door and made straight for the hallway and the stairs down to my warren, when I heard Art call out from the kitchen. "Earl, will you come in here a moment?"

Must be something about work, I thought, something coming up unexpectedly at the store tomorrow. A fashion show, maybe. Happens all the time. But when I rounded the corner and entered the kitchen and saw Art alone in the room, standing by the sink and facing me, his arms crossed limply over his narrow chest, his legs spread as if he would otherwise fall, saw the half-empty bottle of Jim Beam on the counter next to him, I knew what Art had called me in for.

I retreated to the doorway, and he studied me there as if I were of a species other than human, a creature oddly, inexplicably, dressed in human clothes, not a primate, even, and not comical, pathetic—a donkey with trousers. For a long time he examined me, neither of us saying a word, not even swallowing. I knew that I had turned white, and I was suddenly cold, as if an Arctic breeze had blown through the room.

"Do you want a drink of my whiskey?" Art said, his voice

low and old, exhausted, depressed, resigned. His face seemed to have collapsed into itself, like a long-abandoned house into its cellar hole, and his hand, when he reached for the bottle, was trembling, an aged hand, I suddenly noticed, with large brown freckles, bulky knuckles and yellowed fingernails. He was a skinny man, and he'd always seemed dangerously sinewy to me, tall and angular and tough, but now he seemed fragile, off-balance, brittle and moving very carefully, like an old man. I could barely see in him the same man I had cheerfully waved goodbye to four hours earlier at the store, a man who had seemed like an older brother to me, or maybe a young father. This man was ancient, an ancestor, and here he was face to face with his descendant, a fresh-faced boy, healthy, strong, full of blood and muscle—and unutterably callow, a creature so unlike his ancestor that it was as if evolution had reversed itself.

To his offer of whiskey I shook my head no, like a child. "You sure?"

I nodded.

"Well, that's too bad," he said. "That's a real shame. 'Cause I been waiting here for you, thinking we could have us a little whiskey and a little talk, you an' me. Know what I mean, son?" He sounded real Georgian, more so than usual, a country man keeping his thoughts to himself, a trickster. Except that the sadness that covered him like a shroud made him seem frightening. And frightened of him, instead of ashamed of myself, I did not know what to say, so I said nothing at all.

"Here, c'mon over here," he said, and he grabbed up the bottle and pointed with it toward the breakfast nook. "You slide yourself in there opposite me, Earl, so's I can take a good look at you. I want to see you up close for a change. Here I been working and living alongside you for close to a year now, and I ain't had me a good look at you."

I obeyed and slid into the booth and placed my hands on the table.

Art moved in across from me, set the bottle and a glass down before him and said, "How old're you, Earl?"

"Nineteen."

"Nineteen years old. That's about what I thought." He poured an inch of bourbon into his glass and drank half. "Know how old I am?"

"No. Not exactly."

"Not exactly, eh?" Art nipped at his whiskey as if it were hot, and he seemed to be thinking suddenly of something new, a lost memory unexpectedly retrieved. He furrowed his narrow, high brow and said, "I'm almost forty, Earl. Thirty-eight. That's exactly twice as old as you. I got bad knees from basketball and an ulcer since when I was practically your age, back up in Macon, but I expect I can still rip your lungs out, if I want to. You care to contest that, Earl?" he asked delicately.

I wobbled my head back and forth. "No. No, I . . . I don't."

"How old you think Donna is, Earl? Not that it makes one damn bit of difference."

"Look, Art," I said, and I opened my hands as if to reveal a message that would save me. "Look, I . . . ."

"You shut up, son," Art said in a low voice. "You shut your goddamned mouth, and if I ask you a question, you just answer it to the best of your little ability, and that's all. You understand, boy?"

I nodded up and down. Not since my father left had anyone spoken to me that way.

"I asked you a question."

"Yes. Yes, I understand."

"Fine." He seemed to smile, like a snake, quickly, and then it was gone. He poured himself another inch of bourbon, and when he lighted a Chesterfield, I noticed, his hands shook. I looked down at my own hands. They seemed asleep or dead, dogs lying by a fire. A great peace had settled over me, unexplainable, necessary, healing, like a warm and soothing light after long, turbulent darkness. I could not understand it or name its source, but felt under no obligation to do so. That was its nature.

Art's mouth trembled, and he brought his face forward toward mine. "Boy," he said to me, "you have done got yourself caught messin' around where you don't belong. An old, old story, ain't it?"

"Yes."

"Not to you, though. It's a new story to you. Right?"

"Yes. Right."

He looked at me as if my face caused him physical pain. "Well, it's an old story to me," he said. "That's why I'm not mad at you. I should be, but I'm not."

"You're not?" I felt my chest tighten with anxiety.

"No. You're too young and too stupid, I guess. Too trivial, and you don't even know it. You're just an interchangeable part, Earl, that's all. I'm not even mad at Donna. She can't help anything. She's just who she is, that's all, and I know who she is. Always have. So it's *me* who makes me want to puke. For putting up with it. Well," he said, and he sighed and grimaced. "It's all over now, ain't it?"

"Jeez, Art, don't talk that way. I mean . . ."

"Just shut the hell up, will you, Earl?"

"Sorry."

"You're lucky, you know. At first, when she told me she'd been screwing you, I guess I wanted to blow your brains out, all right, which is pretty much what she wanted me to do, or she wouldn't have volunteered the information. That's how she does it, tells me about somebody she's been screwing behind my back and then sits back and watches me come apart. Puts a little spice in her life, I guess. But it don't work anymore. Even that don't work anymore." He was silent for a moment. Then he said, looking straight at me, "My daddy would've shot you and cut off your dick. And he would've shot the woman too. Donna. But he was a better man than I am," he said. He poured himself another shot and studied the glass for a few seconds. "No, that's not true, I'm just feeling sorry for myself. Truth is, I don't really care. About any of it."

"You don't?"

"Yeah. Haven't cared for years. Maybe never. She was always a bitch, and I was always scared of her. It was an ugly marriage from the start. No kids, even. Kids would've made a difference. I would've cared then. But she never wanted none, kept putting it off, kept saying she was too young, which in a sense is true. Anyhow, fact is, she's gone, and I don't give a damn."

"Hell, Art, maybe . . ."

"Earl? Are you listening to me? I'm telling you something here, something I want you to remember tomorrow and next year and on down the line. I'm not telling you because I happen to like you, understand. The opposite, in fact. I just want you to *know* that you ain't the cause of anything, boy. In my life, you're an interchangeable part. In Donna's life, you're an interchangeable part. So whatever happened, whatever happens from here on out, it ain't because of you. You're too puny," he said, pushing his index finger against my chest, "to make a man miserable or ruin a damned marriage that was already ruined anyhow. It was ruined at the start, like most bad marriages. You're too puny. Memorize it, son."

"Where's . . . where's Donna now?"

"Gone. She done flew the coop. Took off for her ma's up in Jacksonville, once she had her fun. Told me what she thought of me, which included telling me about you, since that's a big part of what she thinks of me, and I told her the same as I'm telling you. That I don't care about any of it. Never did. I been just going through the motions all these years. So if you forget about how unimportant you are in the big scheme of things, as you might, since you're a decent kid, you just ask Donna. You might someday want to think you mattered here, but Donna will tell you different."

We were both silent for a moment. Art drank, I clasped

and unclasped my hands, swallowed, opened my mouth to ask the questions I needed answered but couldn't quite form, questions such as "What kind of person does what I have done?"

Instead, I said, "I'm really glad you're not upset . . . about me and Donna and all. I really am in love with Eleanor Hastings, see—"

"Jesus Christ!" he cried. "Will you get the hell away from me! I never should've called you in here. I got nothing to say to you. Nothing." He waved me away with his large, trembling hand. "Go on," he said. *"Git!"*

I got up from the table, and he repeated his command, as if I were an unpleasant dog. *"Git!"*

"I . . . I don't know what to say, Art. Except I'm sorry. I really am sorry."

"No. You ain't sorry one tiny bit. Except for getting caught. And that ain't sorry. But I don't care. So don't even bother saying it. You'll only grow up believing it, and that'll make you worse than a liar. Just shut your damned puny mouth and go on to someplace else real quick. Find yourself a new place to live tomorrow. And on Monday, start looking for a new job. You hear me?" He stared up at me, a sea beast surfacing, tears streaming over his long face, mouth gaping, eyes wild and suffering from a pain I was not even able to be frightened of. Though I could open my eyes and see it, I could not imagine it. And I could not imagine his pain because I refused to know what I had done to him.

It was twelve hours later, nearly midday, when, driving north toward Tampa in my shuddering old Studebaker on my way out to pick up Eleanor, as we'd planned, I was at last able to ask my question and answer it. Not fully, of course, and not even very clearly—I heard both question and answer as if through a wall, a muffled and ambiguous message from the lives of strangers.

I was coming up on a stop sign and glanced into the rear-view mirror and saw my own eyes looking back, only, for the first time, they weren't my eyes, they were my father's, an adult male's blue eyes, scared and secretive, angry and guilt-ridden, eyes utterly without innocence. And instantly, they became the eyes of the whole species, belonging as much to Art and Donna as to my father and mother, and to Eleanor Hastings's father and mother as well, and even, in the end, to me and to the woman I planned to marry. I saw in that moment that every terrible wound they had suffered I could inflict, and every terrible wound they could inflict I could suffer—abandonment, betrayal, deceit, all of them. Our sins describe us, and our prohibitions describe our sins. I had broken them all, I knew, every one. I was a human being, too, at last, and not a very good one, either, weaker, dumber, less imaginative than the good ones.

The breath went out of me and then returned, and immediately my mind filled with images of flight. That's the kind of man I was. I would return to the apartment, toss the few boxes I'd already packed and my duffel into my car, cash a bad check at the corner grocery store and head north into Georgia and the Carolinas, or better, west, toward places like Arkansas and Oklahoma, places where American killers had been disappearing for centuries, fleeing not so much the law as themselves.

I drew the shaky car off the road to the right and shut off the motor and listened to it tick as it cooled. On both sides of the road was a marshland, treeless with clumps of palmettos growing alongside the ditches. The sun beat down on the car, and a slow, hot breeze cut through the open window, while I sat, hands in my lap, sweating and wondering what to do. I had no idea what to do with myself now, for I had never before regarded myself as a bad man, and now I did. Merely to feel guilty, I knew, was so insufficient a response to my new knowledge as to be practically a denial of the facts. I should have understood everything before last night, I thought. For the first time, I was afraid of the consequences of my acts in the right way, beyond guilt, but it was too late. I'd already become the person I should have been afraid of becoming.

Barely a mile away, Eleanor Hastings awaited me. I'd called her first thing that morning and told her only that I'd quarreled with Art over money and was going to move out of his house and would have to find a new job right away, so our plans to spend the afternoon at my place would have to be canceled. "But only temporary, honey," I assured her.

How would *she* respond to the facts? I wondered—for I knew I would tell her everything, about my committing adultery and about my talk with Art last night. I'd tell her about all the other laws I'd broken too, all the lying, stealing, and cheating I'd done, all the envy and covetousness, all the dishonor. I'd say to her, "Here! *This* is what's been hidden from you, this is what I've hidden from myself." I would show her who I was, and then I would ask her if she still wanted to marry me. And if she was foolish and desperate enough to say yes, I was ready to reward her by blinding myself to the most important fact of all, for I also knew at that moment in my car by the side of the road in North St. Petersburg, knew it on a Sunday afternoon in September of 1959 as well as I know it now a quarter century later, that I did not love Eleanor Hastings then, or before, and would not love her after we were married in January.

I turned the key in the ignition, and the old Studebaker coughed and caught, and a few moments later I pulled into the driveway of the home of the parents of my bride-to-be. She ran out the door, smiling, arms open, to greet me.

Hostage

1

Jan is the first to realize what is about to happen, and he begins to shout, running frantically from the living room down the narrow hallway to the stairs, scrambling up the stairs to the room with the skylight, where the others—Eva, Deke, Odum and Schmidt, the ambassador—are seated on the floor in a square playing a four-sided game with black and white pebbles.

They hear him coming, hear him shriek the alarm, roar out their names, and when he bursts through the door, they meet him by shouting, all four of them, even Schmidt, angry, full of panic, bewildered. After a few seconds of bedlam, Jan's high-pitched voice again dominates, and though there are still no explanations, he is swiftly allowed by the others to give orders and have them swiftly followed.

He tells Odum to stay in the room with Schmidt and to bolt the door on the inside when they have gone out, to barricade it with the several pieces of furniture in the room and not to open it again until he hears the password from one of the other three.

Then, before leaving the room, Jan has Deke break out

a German handgun and twelve dozen rounds of ammunition from the chest at the top of the stairs, which he hands to Odum, instructing him not to fire the gun until or unless he can use it to kill a man. "Don't open the skylight, don't draw any attention to this room. Use the gun only if the door is broken open! Kill whoever breaks it open!" he barks.

"What about Schmidt?" Odum asks in a low voice, holding the weapon loosely in his left hand, the small yellow carton of ammunition in his right.

Jan doesn't answer. He yells at Deke to get the hell downstairs with one of the automatic rifles and a case of ammunition for Eva at the kitchen window. Roughly shoving Eva on the shoulder, he says to her, "Go *on,* this is *it.* You take the kitchen window, Deke and I'll be at the front." Then he runs after them, down the stairs three steps at a time.

Odum quickly closes the door and throws the bolt and starts shoving the dresser, chair and cot against the door. When he is finished, he sits down against the far wall, opposite Schmidt, cradling the pistol in his two hands as if it is the corpse of a small gray cat. Across from him, Schmidt breathes heavily but peacefully, a middle-aged man about to take an afternoon nap.

Downstairs, Eva protects the back of the house, the wide lawn that gives way to a meadow. Jan and Deke in the living room squat beneath windows that face downhill and across the yard to the birches and the road. The house falls silent.

"*There!* By the birches, on the right!" Jan says, aiming his M-16 out the open window, shoving the dark tip of the barrel several inches beyond the sill. A gray-uniformed figure darts behind a half-dozen birch trees, his image fragmenting, as light by a prism, and quickly disappears. "There's a bunch of 'em behind the birch grove," Jan whispers.

Deke nods silently, craning to see what has disappeared, seeing nothing from his position, until a flash of gray on his left, from behind the car parked down on the road, yanks his gaze away from the birches and fixes it directly in front of him. "Somebody's behind our car," he announces. "I'll take him out next time he shows."

"No, wait till they make their move," Jan orders. "No, go ahead, get the bastard! They've already made their move."

Deke obediently squeezes the trigger, firing off ten or twelve sudden rounds, and the gray figure standing behind the hood of the green American sedan flips around and bounces onto the dirt road, bleeding large scarlet bubbles from the throat and lower face. Two men run from the birch grove toward the fallen figure by the car and Jan starts firing, killing both men before they reach the shelter of the car. Gunfire explodes at the back of the house, a barrage, Eva firing short bursts in answer. Then a fusillade opens up from the birch grove in front, shattering all the glass in the windows, splintering wood and crumbling plaster inside, flinging shreds of the curtains into the room as if by invisible hands. Deke and Jan are now firing without pause, except to slam a fresh clip into place, firing again, emptying the clip, ejecting it and slamming in a fresh one, firing again. Jan slips, turns his ankle and falls to the floor. Jamming a fresh clip into his weapon, he looks up and over and sees Deke slide down onto the floor, a hole the size of his own huge fist in the middle of his face, the area from his mouth to his eyebrows filling with dark red blood. Then, looking up to the doorway that leads to the kitchen, Jan sees Eva walk stiffly into the room, hands flopping loosely at her sides, as if trying to shake off leeches, her dark eyes rolling back into her head, her mouth and teeth chewing the air, a bloody orchid spreading swiftly between her breasts as she crumples at the knees and falls face-first onto the floor.

Jan looks out the window one last time and sees the yard flood with armed men in gray uniforms. They are charging from the road to the house, halfway there now, a hundred guns hurtling fire ahead of them. Without hesitation, Jan kicks off one shoe, jams the barrel of his gun into his mouth, and with his big toe, squeezes the trigger. The door to the house comes crashing in and in seconds the room is filled with dozens of angry, milling, shouting men who, clutching their weapons, poke at the three corpses with the tips of black boots, roll them over, study the faces with anger and disgust.

2

Plan A

Three of us make a run into the city, Deke, Jan, and me, Deke driving, me sitting in front next to him, Jan in the back. Jan is jabbering continuously, whether we listen or not. Bumming cigarettes from Deke, he is trying, as always, to apply the theories and teachings of his leaders to the lives, to the pains, pleasures, deprivations and fantasies, of every human being he has known, seen or sees now as we glide in the big green car along the causeway into the city.

The city is crisp today, seems almost new beneath the wind-washed cold blue sky. Along the sidewalks, everyone moves briskly inside overcoats and scarves, bright-faced people puffing small clouds of breath before them. Jan is telling us how, when the air of summer, finally, *inevitably* (for Jan, *everything* is inevitable), becomes too heavily laden with industrial filth for the winter rains to wash it clean, when that happens, the people will have to give up this last delusion and the respite it provides. "And then you'll see some action," he promises us.

Deke farts slowly, switches a toothpick from one corner of his loose red mouth to the other. He snorts through hairy nostrils, as if remembering something funny, and stops the car at an intersection. A traffic officer stands at the center of the intersection, facing us down with upheld white-gloved hand, his black holster and the belt around his thick waist suddenly dominating our field of vision. The hammer and handle of the gun and the holster shine dully blue in the pale morning sunlight.

A throng of shoppers and workers, clerk types clutching newspapers and briefcases, hustles across the street in front of us, when suddenly, pointing left, reaching between Deke's nose and the dashboard, with my index finger rigidly extended, as if pushing a button, I say, "My God, is that who I think it is?"

Deke and Jan quickly gaze in the direction I am pointing, into the glut of anonymous faces and hurrying bodies, and as Jan, with rising intensity, whines, "What the hell are you talking about, Schmidt? *Who?*" I yank open the door beside me, step out, slam it shut behind me and dash into the crowd of people flowing swiftly around the front of the car to the right side of the street.

Reaching the sidewalk safely, I stop in my flight and face the traffic officer, diagonally across from me. "Officer!"

He notices me, his curiosity pricked by my loud, ambiguous call from this slight distance. Dropping his gloved hand, he waves for the line of cars to continue on. He waves again, this time with annoyance, as Deke hesitates to move the car ahead.

"Officer!" I repeat.

"C'mon, Mac, get the lead out!" he snarls at Deke, whose puzzled round face peers through the windshield, first at the traffic officer, then at me, then back over his shoulder at Jan, who, crimson-faced, is shouting soundless orders at him. Then, at last, the car pulls ahead, passes through the intersection and moves slowly down the street, Jan's dark red face glowering back at me from the rear window.

"Whaddaya want, Mac?" the officer says, casting a final, irritated glance at Deke and Jan.

I take a careful step or two off the sidewalk onto the street. "I . . . I have a heart condition, officer. I'm feeling . . . faint. Where should I go, can you help me?"

He claps a beefy hand on my shoulder, and I smile wanly into his broad, paternal face. "You want oxygen?" he asks in a low voice, as if offering contraband.

"Yes."

"Okay, pal. Just go on over to the wagon there, right there, halfway down the block, and tell the officer there, he's sitting inside in back, just tell him I sent you down for a shot of oxygen. Think you can make it that far all right?"

"Yes, yes . . . I think so." I turn and start slowly away, turn back for a second, smiling weakly. "Officer? Thank you. You've just saved my life."

He grins expansively, waves me on my way and strides proudly back to the center of the intersection, as I slowly, with great care, walk down the block to the blue station wagon.

The oxygen is delightful, a genuine lift. Hoo boy, I'm *free!* (Like that.) Twelve hours later, I'm recently arrived in a small town in the mountains of the north, signing a new name in the register of a run-down rooming house located two tree-lined blocks off the almost deserted main street. The soft, round-topped mountains loom darkly around the town. The sky, like a rose-colored plate, glides swiftly, with serenity, before the oncoming night. I talk all evening with the landlady and the other roomers about how I've had to come here for my health. We talk slowly and drink tea and rock in our wicker chairs. Not bad. Safe.

Plan B

I become two people. Easy. It happens while I am sleeping and while the others are asleep also. The house lies in total darkness—a moonless night, overcast, the still air laced by the rough brushings of the bare branches of the birch trees around the house. I am wearing an elaborate disguise, a black curly wig that makes me look Greek or possibly Arabic, with a thick mustache, also black. My teeth have been stained tobacco brown, my complexion dimmed with theatrical makeup, and I am wearing a dark green mechanic's shirt and trousers, with *Rollo* sewn to the flap of my left breast pocket, *Schumann's Garage* on the other. My pockets are filled with tools—pliers, screwdrivers, a file, a flashlight, et cetera—and my hands are stained with grease, as if I have been fishing through the innards of an automobile engine. As a final touch, I cover my blue eyes with brown-tinted, wire-rimmed eyeglasses and find myself standing in the center of a darkened room, a natural-born auto mechanic sent out tonight on an emergency call by Chub Schumann. I have not much of the language yet, which is why I am the one who, in addition to working six days a week, must be on standby for emergencies six nights a week. But I don't mind. I want to make good and become foreman.

Guiding my steps with the beam of my flashlight, I cross to the cot in the corner. I pull a screwdriver from my pocket and plunge it straight down into the sleeping man's heart, Odum's, probably, letting go of it at once and clapping my hand over his wildly open mouth to stifle any possible last cry. Then, sliding the screwdriver back out, wiping it off with a greasy rag from my back pocket, I walk quickly to the door at the opposite side of the room, and with the same screwdriver, carefully spring the latch without breaking the lock.

I crack open the door and check the hallway outside. Darkness, silence. Then I am outside the room, closing the door soundlessly behind me, carefully leaving it locked. No one discovers or even delays me as I stroll from the house, jump the crushed-stone walkway to the grass and hike the dirt road three miles to the main road, where Schumann's Garage, like a deserted concrete bunker, squats behind two Epco gas pumps. It takes me a moment to jump the ignition wires of the battered blue German pickup truck that's parked next to the garage, and ten minutes later—the red beacon flashing from the top of the cab, headlights splashing chalky light across the frost-covered lawn and the bulky green Oldsmobile sedan parked outside—I have pulled up in front of the house. I leave the motor running, the red light flashing madly. Stepping from the truck, I crunch along the walk to the front door of the farmhouse and bang on the door with wonderful abandon.

Lights go on all over the house—but not, of course, in the room upstairs, the room with the skylight. After a few seconds, the door is opened halfway. It's Jan. Shirtless, barefoot, his trousers only partially buttoned, thin black wisps of hair sticking out from his narrow head like a dark crown accentuating the startled expression that swarms across his face. Wide-eyed, his mouth open and stammering, he finally gets a question out. "What . . . what's the matter, whaddaya want?"

"You got trouble. Right?" I am grimly serious. Businesslike. "Schumann's Garage. That the one?" I ask, pointing with my chin in the general direction of the Oldsmobile. With the house lights on, Jan and I both can see Schumann's pickup and can read the bright red and white lettering along the side: *24 Hour Emergency Service & Towing.*

"What the hell are you talking about, fella?" Jan says to me, his face tightening into that fist it makes when he gets angry or is confused. Tonight he is both.

"Somebody here called. For getting the car started." Stolid, unsubtle foreigner.

Jan rubs his head in puzzlement, then suddenly shoots a look behind him and yells, "Deke! Check upstairs!" He turns quietly back to me. "Listen, fella, somebody's made a mistake. Was it a *man* called you, anybody you know or maybe could recognize?" he asks in a patronizing voice, that greasy, false, utterly illegitimate voice of his.

"Naw. Mister Chub Schumann calls me. The phone for the night emergency is over at his house. I am only the mechanic for at night, you know. Mister Schumann, he always tells me when to go out and when to forget it, stay sleeping." I grin brown rotted teeth at him, dousing him with garlic breath. "Maybe Mister Schumann made a big mistake tonight. Some other one lives here, maybe? Maybe that one called for help to get started?" I'm trying to be helpful.

Deke, jamming his shirttail into his pants, appears at the bottom of the stairs behind Jan, white-faced, horrified, his red mouth gray from the shock. He grabs Jan's elbow and whispers into his ear. As if my face were next to theirs, as close as a lover leaning to kiss his beloved on the lips, I hear Deke say to Jan, "Odum, he's dead."

Jan lifts his upper lip in a dry snarl. "Schmidt?"

"Still there. Sleeping."

Jan's face goes slack with puzzlement, then tightens with fear again. "Who . . . ?"

"The door was locked from the inside, as always," Deke adds.

Jan turns to me and growls, "Nobody here called you, buddy. Nobody. So take off," he snaps, closing the door, clicking the lock on the other side.

I roll across to the truck on the balls of my feet, a broad smile spreading over my face. Climbing into the truck, I flick off the red beacon, back the truck out to the road, and drive away.

In less than an hour, I'm in another province. I don't desert the truck until daylight, and by that time I'm in yet another province. I leave it in a shopping center parking lot in front of a men's clothing store. After breakfast, I'll be able to pick up some clothes there, a suitcase from the leather goods shop next to it, and across the street, in the men's room of the filling station, I'll wash, shave and change clothes. I glimpse a long-distance bus as it hisses to a gradual stop in front of a small yellow-brick building a short ways beyond the filling station. Great. By noon at the latest, I'll have made my escape. I'll tell wonderful lies to the person sitting next to me.

Plan C

I become three people. Two of the people burst into the house on a night when Deke and I have been left behind, a night when the others—Jan, Eva, and Odum—have made

a quick run into the city to attend a Regional Group Leader-
ship Seminar. Deke is quickly overpowered, shot full of
lorazepam (so that later, when he has been told I've been
rescued, he will recall nothing that will betray my rescuers),
and the three of us hurry into the night, laughing, slapping
each other on the back. Together again!

Who would've thought it possible?

Plan D

I pray to a god, fasting while I pray, mortifying my
flesh during this period, a week, then two weeks, a fortnight,
with my face pressed constantly against the floor, the bones
of my face, as they gradually shove through tissue to skin,
bruising from the unbroken force of my prayer, until, at last,
on the twenty-seventh day, the god touches my spine and
I am made invisible even to my own eyes, invisible and lifted
through the roof across the lawn to the woods and down to
the spongy, moss-covered stump of an ancient oak, where
I am made visible again, so that I may watch myself as I fall
forward onto my face, to resume my prayer to the god, this
time a prayer of thanksgiving.

Plan E (a desperate last resort)

A complex, utterly secret plan (secret even from myself) culminates with my slaying everyone in the house and
burying the bodies under the gravel walkway, one at a time
and immediately after each killing, while the body is still
warm, until I am finally forced to realize that I am the only
one left. I try calling the murders "escape" and my solitude
"freedom." I try and I try, but consistently I fall into confu-
sion.

3

Except for the crunch of their boots against the floor
and the squeak and clank of weapons, the soldiers and the

several officers hear nothing. No groans, no cries for help, no stammered, frantic surrenders, none of the sounds they would expect to hear after a fierce battle has been won. Before them, torn and bleeding slowly onto the bare floor, lie the bodies of Jan, Deke and Eva. A young blond lieutenant pushes his way through the crowd of gray-uniformed soldiers that has formed around the corpses, sending the men to the sides of the room. He gets down on one knee next to Jan's destroyed face, grimaces with disgust and goes quickly through his pockets. A roll of paper money, some change, American cigarettes and a butane lighter, a Swiss army knife, a plastic comb and a passport with Jan's picture and physical description and the name *Swim Nagle*—nothing else.

"Check out the rest of the house," the lieutenant orders, and immediately the soldiers start to scurry through the downstairs rooms, ransacking closets, cabinets, bureaus, emptying the contents onto the floors as they go. Most of the soldiers are young, not yet twenty, and they grin with curiosity and evident relief while they work.

After having searched the pockets of Deke and Eva, both of whom are dressed in khaki blouses and trousers, the lieutenant stands up and with a slender baton points at four of the soldiers, men slightly older than the others, probably professionals. "You four," he says crisply. "Check upstairs. Our informant says there's only one room up there. Some kind of attic. If anyone's up there, remember, he's in a corner. Be careful. Don't worry about the ambassador, he's surely long gone. They expected this."

The four nod and start slowly up the stairs, single file, weapons ready.

Behind them, a colonel, followed by his driver, has just entered the living room and now is being apprised of the situation by the young lieutenant. Both officers look grim but somewhat bored.

"Are these three the lot of 'em?" the colonel asks. He is

a ruddy-faced man, gray-haired, about fifty-five, with a mustache and slightly overweight, dressed in an impeccable uniform festooned with war ribbons. "I'd expected more of the bastards."

"From the firepower, so did I. But it all came from down here, sir. And they were well armed," the lieutenant points out, touching a black-booted toe to the stock of Deke's M-16. As his toe reaches the weapon, the hard, flat sound of a gunshot flies through the house. Everyone swings around to the stairs, and the four grizzled soldiers who went up come suddenly scrambling back down to the first landing, where, before anyone else can react, they regroup and charge back up, three steps at a time. When they reach the top, a second shot goes off, and the four run, two abreast, down the hallway toward the door at the end, hurtling the combined bulk of their bodies against the door, smashing it with shoulders and ejecting them into the room, weapons ready to fill the small space with gunfire.

The force of their entry scatters the few pieces of furniture that were stacked against the door, spilling the bureau, cot and chair into the several corners of the room. In the exact center of the room lie the bodies of two men. One is middle-aged and heavier than the other. Both men are dressed in the plain khaki blouse and trousers of the three downstairs. Both men are dead.

One of the soldiers walks back to the head of the stairs and calls down. "It's all right, sir! There were two of them up here. Both dead now."

The lieutenant follows the colonel up the stairs at a respectful distance, enters the room slightly behind him and notes with surprise that both bodies are bleeding profusely from the mouth. A closer look leads him to surmise that both men shot themselves. Presumably, the younger man went first, then the older man. His left hand still clutches the stock of the German pistol. Later on, powder burns on the older man (eventually identified as Schmidt, the ambassador) will support the lieutenant's controversial conjecture that he did, indeed, take his own life, as did the other, somewhat younger man, a person identified finally as Odum, a member of The Group.

Mistake

In the spring of 1960 I turned twenty. By June I'd be married, so I was working at a second job, selling women's shoes at a Thom McAn's in a shopping center out in West St. Petersburg. Driving home late six nights a week in my shaky '48 Studebaker, I cast wary glances out the open window at the causeway that loped across the bay north to Tampa, a string of lights over dark water that somehow made me think of New York City, and for a few terrifying seconds each night I wondered if I was making the biggest mistake of my life.

Days I worked as a window trimmer for Webb's City, after I'd been let go at Maas Brothers. It was an early cut-rate department store parked on an invisible line that separated the neighborhood where middle-class blacks lived from the neighborhood where poor whites lived. There were eight of us in the Display Department, as it was called—art school dropouts, alcoholic ex-stagehands, sign painters and me—and from the small warehouse on the edge of the Webb's City parking lot where we toiled through the long, hot Florida day building frames, cutting and stretching paper, carving Homosote, painting signs, repairing old mannequins, we looked out the open door one way and watched the black people stroll their streets, turned and looked out the door on the opposite side and watched the white people, mostly runaway Georgia farmers and their wives and skinny children, pass their days on the broken-down porches of rented bungalows.

It could have been depressing, but I was twenty years old and going to be married soon to a very pretty eighteen-year-old blond girl with green eyes that made me feel crazy. Also, I was thought to be unusually talented at this business of decorating department store windows. I had a future. When you think you have a future, you're not easily depressed.

My roommate at the time, Martin Schram, who worked with me at Webb's City, did not think he had a future. He was thirty-one, had spent two years in Cleveland studying art, then had joined the navy. He learned to paint signs and after four years on an aircraft carrier went back for four more, until he got frightened by what he seemed to be doing to his life, so he came home to Cleveland, where he found that he'd already done it, and moved to Florida.

We shared a railroad flat that was half a bungalow. Martin, since he was older, claimed the more desirable front room, which had windows and a door to the porch. I got the middle room, which was small and dark, a kind of damp, hot cavern between Martin's room and the kitchen and bath in back. I figured that with my two jobs I wasn't home much anyhow, and besides, by the time I got married to Eleanor I'd have enough money saved up to buy a whole house. As a result, I didn't complain about the darkness and the heat and the occasional slugs that inched their way up the gray walls, fell back to the floor and after a while started over again.

Martin envied me because Eleanor loved me. "I don't mean that I love your Eleanor," he said the night this all came out. "I don't even particularly like her." It was past midnight, a Friday in late April, and I had come home from

Thom McAn's exhausted, as I'd been working five days and nights straight, angry because I still had another to go, and more than usually frightened, for I'd endured an especially horrifying vision of the causeway lights over Tampa Bay on the drive home, had felt my legs turn to water, because the awful question did not go away when I forced my gaze back to the white line in the road ahead of me, and I almost cracked and cried out, Yes, I am certainly about to make the biggest mistake of my life!

We were drinking beer. Colt 45 was new then, and I liked the snow-covered mountains and blue sky on the label, especially when it was hot and like tonight had recently rained and the live oak trees and Spanish moss were still dripping noisily onto the muddy front yard and sidewalk beyond. I stripped as I passed through my room, walked shirtless and barefoot out to the dark kitchen and swung open the refrigerator, let the pale, cool light wash the room, and there on the top shelf, frosty and brilliant, was a pair of unopened six-packs of blue, white, and gold cans of beer.

By the time he told me he envied me, Martin and I had finished the first six-pack and were halfway through the second. Martin Schram could drink beer. He was German and thick-bodied, built like an overstuffed sofa. He had dark, short hair that he was losing, a heavy brow and large, square chin, and a grim, thin mouth. His blue eyes, though small, were the most expressive and easily read part of his face, and when I wanted to know what he was thinking, which wasn't all that often, I looked at his eyes. Tonight, however, we were out on the unlit porch, bare feet on the wooden rail, seated side by side in plastic-and-aluminum folding chairs, and I could not see his eyes and had to ask him what he meant.

He sighed.

"No, I mean it. What do you mean, you envy me because of Eleanor?"

"Forget it, kid," he said. He emptied the can and

crunched it with one hand. The lightweight aluminum cans had just come out then, and we liked smashing them as if they were the rigid cans that took two hands to crush.

"Kid," I said.

That's when the noise next door started. A man and woman lived there, the Smiths, known to me and Martin only by the name on the mailbox on the door next to ours and by sight, when they went out to work in the morning and returned at night. They spent the rest of the time inside their apartment, no matter how hot it got, which left the porch entirely to us, a circumstance we did not complain of. We figured they stayed inside because the man was deformed. Mr. Smith's arms were like flippers, half as long as normal arms and dwindled at the wrists and hands. Evidently, he was able to drive, and judging from the way he dressed—sport coat altered specially for his arms, slacks, dress shirt and tie—he held a decent job. Mrs. Smith was normal-looking. Actually, she was on the attractive side (as was he, except for the arms) and went out every morning dressed like a salesgirl at a first-class department store, Maas Brothers, say, a place that wouldn't hire any of the short, dumpy, gum-chewing, acne-covered women and girls who could get work at Webb's City. Eleanor worked at Maas Brothers, in beachwear.

We'd heard noises from next door on several occasions that year, always late at night, and always Friday, payday. It was the sound of a man beating a woman. More precisely, it was the sound of a woman hollering that she was being beaten by a man, something we, of course, discounted, because we could not imagine how he could do it. There'd be a thump and a bang or two, then a shriek, a wail, some long drawn-out sobs, some more thumps, then quiet. That was it. Martin would look over at me, if we both happened to be home and in the same room at the time, and he'd shake his head and smile. "Sonofabitch's at it again."

"Yeah. Can't really be hurting her, though."

"No. She's as big as he is, and she's got regular arms."

"Yeah. It's just probably something they do."

"Yeah. You can never tell what people like."

"Yeah."

This time, though, was different. The noises went on too long, and they got louder. Mr. Smith sounded drunk, and we could hear him snapping and snarling like a dog in a dogfight, and she was wailing, a high, unbroken keening sort of sound, as if she were an old Greek woman who'd been told her favorite son was dead.

"Jesus Christ," Martin said. "They're really going at it tonight."

"What do you think?" I said. I got up from my chair and walked across the porch and faced the closed door to their apartment. "Maybe the bastard's hitting her with a stick or something."

"Naw, they're like a coupla alley cats, that's all. Forget it." I heard him crack open another beer. Three left. If I didn't open a fresh one now, he'd get two and I'd get one. But then I'd have two warm beers instead of one cold one. Hard to choose.

"I don't know, I think we oughta do something," I said.

"Like what? Call the cops? I don't believe in that. Husband and wife, they got to work these things out themselves. You'll see."

I opened the screened door to our apartment and went back to the kitchen and got myself a cold beer. When I came out to the porch, I put the unopened can on the floor next to my chair and went on drinking the open one.

Then Mrs. Smith started screaming, "No, no, no!" Mr. Smith's voice was muffled, but it sounded like he was threatening to kill her, over and over.

"I think he's trying to kill her," I said.

"No," Martin said, but he got up from his chair and joined me in front of their door.

"What if he's got a gun?"

"I don't think the bastard can shoot it. All he's got is those little grippers, for Christ's sake."

"The sonofabitch can drive a car!"

"Yeah."

"You think we should do something?" I asked.

"No. He's just a crippled little guy taking it out on his wife. It's just something they do," Martin said, and he moved slowly away and down the steps to the front yard.

"Where you going?"

"I want to see if maybe I can see inside," he said from the darkness. "They got all the blinds drawn."

"I heard a gun!"

"What? I didn't hear it."

"No, a click. I heard it click, like maybe he's only clicking it at her. You know?"

Martin came back onto the porch and sat himself heavily into the folding chair. "If the gun goes off, then I'll worry. Not before." He took a long pull from his beer. "Clicks." He laughed lightly.

Mrs. Smith screamed, and I reached forward and pushed the doorbell. Silence on the other side of the door. I waited a few seconds and pushed the bell again, a long, loud buzz, and slowly the door opened, and I saw Mr. Smith standing there in T-shirt and slacks, panting, red-faced, without a gun.

"What do you want?" He was several inches shorter than I and slender, almost delicate-looking. His lank blond hair had fallen across his face, and his mouth was working angrily, as if trying to rid itself of something objectionable. His tiny, shriveled arms hung at his sides like the wings of a newly hatched bird. He looked pathetic, but very angry, and I was surprised by finding myself afraid of him, afraid of his intensity, actually, his breathlessness and flushed face and hard eyes, the desperation these things signified to me. I had none of it, and until that moment I had not known it even existed in the world, despite the signals I had been getting every night on my drive home from the shoestore. And despite

Martin Schram, whose envy of me I understood so feebly that I could barely hide my lack of interest.

"We heard a lotta noise," I said gruffly.

He looked me over with care, without apology. "You trying to sleep?"

"No . . . but we were wondering . . ."

"Who's that?" Mrs. Smith called from somewhere behind him. I could see furniture overturned beyond the man, rugs rippled and out of place, an empty quart beer bottle, still rolling. The light in the room cut a blond swath across the far wall at an oblique, useless angle, as if a table lamp had been placed on its side on the floor. I imagined Mrs. Smith lying in a corner of the room, holding mournfully to her rib cage, her legs splayed out in front of her, and I forgot my fear and was glad I had interrupted them.

"The kid next store," Mr. Smith said, as if disappointed.

"Are you all right?" I called.

"Get the hell out of here," he said. "Mind your own damn business."

I drew open the screened door. "Are you all right, Mrs. Smith?"

She entered the living room from the darkness of the room beyond and leaned against the doorframe there, wearing a filmy pink nightgown, her bare arms crossed over her breasts, her legs crossed at the ankles. She looked bored, impatient, irritated, all at once.

I took a single step toward her and, halfway into the room, said to her, "I'm sorry. I just . . . I thought he . . ."

Suddenly, the man was shoving me back with his tiny arms, pushing them against my chest, astonishing me with the hard force of the shoves. "Get outa here! G'wan, get outa here!"

I leapt out of his way and yelled, "Leave her alone, you sonofabitch! Leave the woman alone!"

Then Martin was behind me, grabbing me from behind and yanking me away from the door.

"Close your door!" he said to Smith. "And shut the hell up. For God's sake."

Smith closed the door, and Martin turned to me. His face in the brown light off the shaded windows had collapsed in on itself, and I saw him as I'd never seen him before. He was frightened and very sad and deeply, painfully weary of me. His small eyes were watered over, and his thin lips trembled.

I took a step backward, turned, and sat down. Martin came around and sat down next to me, and I could tell, even without looking at him, that his whole body was shaking.

I was very calm. "I'm sorry," I said. I leaned over and plucked the unopened can of Colt 45 from the floor and opened it and took a slug.

"You . . ." he said.

"What?"

"You don't know a damned thing about anything."

"You're right."

"You just say that. You say it so easy," he said. He lit a cigarette. The rain had stopped a long time before, and now the dripping from the trees and Spanish moss had stopped too. Crickets started up. I heard trucks on Route 19, three blocks away, change gears.

"You're right about that too," I said. "I say it so easy." I stood up, leaned against the railing and looked at his silhouette. "But I mean it."

"You probably do," he said, as if he no longer cared. It was too late to matter to him. He got up then and went inside and lay down on his bed and fell asleep.

I did marry the girl, Eleanor with the green eyes, Eleanor from beachwear, and it was not the biggest mistake I ever made, even though it was, of course, a mistake. Two weeks before the wedding, I was hired as display director for the Montgomery Ward's store in Lakeland, youngest display director in the state of Florida, and moved out of the apartment I shared with Martin Schram.

"You better come to the wedding, pal," I said. We were

on the porch, a midafternoon, with a rented trailer behind my Studebaker, all my worldly belongings inside.

"I'll be there," he said, and he clapped me on both shoulders. "You'll be okay."

"You will too," I said.

"Right."

We shook hands, and I left.

Children's Story

The afternoon I tossed Ralph from the roof to the ground and broke him, I thought I was the only father who had ever done such a thing to his child. I was young, but seven years have passed since then, and in those intervening years I have come to know of numerous tossings and breakings that in all but a few insignificant details are identical to mine and Ralph's.

Usually, this is what happens. The father is unexpectedly attacked by the child, often from behind and frequently with a weapon—a paring knife, for example, or the pointed end of a bottle opener. This often occurs when the father is engrossed in watching a sports event on television or reading the newspaper or standing at the bottom of the stairs with the telephone in his hand, about to direct-dial his mother long-distance in California.

Evidently, the child desires from the father a particular kind of attention, and it is because the attack comes precisely when the father's attention is wholly elsewhere that the child is able to incorporate into his attack the element of extreme surprise. Thus armed, his child, like a terrorist, is shockingly dangerous, way out of proportion to his diminutive size. The father, bleeding profusely, is momentarily disabled. He falls to his knees, is perhaps stabbed a second time, looks from his new wound to the child, gaze locking into gaze, for their heads are now at the same low level, and suddenly the father realizes that this combat is no mock duel, that it is instead mortal and that there is no decorum that will not make him vulnerable. Despite their different body weights and technical skills, they are both, however briefly, human beings.

Thus the father chooses a strategy that will save him, purely and simply. Usually he chooses lying. And as soon as the child has been lied into a false sense of security (fulsome protestations of love and concern for the child's welfare, assurances of endless devotion, actual monetary gifts, a plethora of fondling, cooing, stroking of cheeks and patting of little heads—such are the lies), the father sweeps the child from his tiny bed, wraps him in a blanket, races to the roof with his bundle and tosses it to the street below.

That's how it went with me and Ralph, and that's how it's gone for untold hundreds of others. For a brief period after I had tossed my Ralph from the roof, I thought I was an unnatural father, but when I learned of so many similar cases, I was able to go a little easier on myself. My wife, Ralph's mother, was a great help to me in this, but I needed more reassurance than even she could provide. After all, she was my wife, a fellow adult, and was bound to support and comfort me. And, too, there was a sense in which, by having disposed of Ralph myself, I had saved her the obligation to do it. For she, as much as I, had endured the child's sudden attacks, and she, too, was frightened of him and wished to protect herself against him.

Eventually, when I had learned of all the cases that corresponded to mine and my wife's, I came gradually to view parents who passively endured their children's opposition as unnatural parents, as abnormal, as, at best, deeply irrational. They seemed to long for their own destruction, for their own replacement in the world by their children. Men and women like that, I came to believe, were frightening and also a little disgusting. They often claimed to be acting out of instinct, and sometimes they went so far as to insist that by permitting the children to feed on their adult bodies, as it were, they were at the same time enlarging themselves. But I knew by then that they had been deeply deceived by themselves and their children and in actuality were acting out of a perverse and dark impulse to destroy themselves.

Survival of the fittest! I used to shout, when with our neighbors at a cookout or cocktail party the subject of children came up. And it seemed always to come up, probably because as young parents the question of proper attitudes and actions toward children was for us a depressingly real one. Throughout the neighborhood, children had reached the age where they were capable of attacking and mortally wounding their parents, and naturally the parents were worried.

Since most of us were morally conscientious adults, most of us were eager to locate the morally appropriate response to these attacks. Every day we'd hear some new account of a child poking his mother in the eye with a rake handle, another attempting to shove his father into the open door of the furnace in the basement or, one that especially alarmed us, a five-year-old boy who released the handbrake of the family sedan when it was parked on an incline and let it roll down the slope toward the father, who was leaning to remove a roller skate from the driveway. The father had not been able to get out of the way of the car in time and had suffered a smashed ankle and knee and as a consequence was hospitalized for seven weeks and out of work for three months. Even today he walks with a noticeable limp.

We were told about this at a barbecue at our next-door neighbor's home one summer evening right after it happened, and my reaction was to suggest that, as friends and concerned parents, we should appoint a committee to help the disabled father by abducting the child ourselves and throwing him from a nearby turnpike overpass. We should let it serve as a warning to the other children, I urged. We must show them that our loyalties to each other are strong and that we will respond as a group if any one of us is attacked by a child. They'll think twice, I predicted, if they know they'll have forty or fifty well-conditioned adults pouncing on them every time one of them steps out of line.

A few of the women in the group argued against the idea, mainly on the grounds that our action might inspire the children to take collective action as well. They pointed out that since it was the children who were always the instigators of these vicious attacks, we would have no way of knowing when or where the next attack would come from—the paper boy, the child of a friend, a visiting niece or nephew. If we can ally ourselves, one woman argued, so can they, and since our actions are always defensive and in reaction to theirs, we might, with this idea of an alliance, be giving them the means to remove our capacity as individual parents to retaliate and protect ourselves. Your idea, she warned me, might have unexpected long-range consequences. And then she clinched the argument and carried it by pointing out what we all knew and lived with daily but rarely admitted to ourselves.

There are more of them than us, she said in a voice almost a whisper, and suddenly depressed, she sat back into her chair by the pool and stared out across the backyards and hedges in the general direction of the playground, where we could hear in the distance the shrill cries and shrieks of the children at play, could sense their immense numbers and their natural affiliation with each other, their natural enmity to us.

Oh, God, one of the men said in a low voice. What are we going to do?

Just pray that they soon grow up and become adults themselves, my wife answered. Feed and clothe and shelter them, she said, hurry them along, distract them, lie to them, and at all times be vigilant against them. Eventually, if we're lucky and careful, they'll be adults too, and we'll be free. We'll be free, and they'll have become parents, she said with a smile, as she savored the sweet taste of anticipated victory.

I wrapped my arms around my wife's sensible, delicate shoulders and shared the vision with her for a few seconds, knowing that we both were picturing our daughter Amy, born three years after Ralph, as a mother. Then, arm in arm, we bid good night to our hosts and in the gathering dusk strolled across the lawn to our house and went in and drew the blinds in our bedroom and made long and sweetly satisfying love again.

Sarah Cole: A Type of Love Story

1

To begin, then, here is a scene in which I am the man and my friend Sarah Cole is the woman. I don't mind describing it now, because I'm a decade older and don't look the same now as I did then, and Sarah Cole is dead. That is to say, on hearing this story you might think me vain if I looked the same now as I did then, because I must tell you that I was extremely handsome then. And if Sarah were not dead, you'd think I was cruel, for I must tell you that Sarah was very homely. In fact, she was the homeliest woman I have ever known. Personally, I mean. I've *seen* a few women who were more unattractive than Sarah, but they were clearly freaks of nature or had been badly injured or had been victimized by some grotesque, disfiguring disease. Sarah, however, was quite normal, and I knew her well, because for three and a half months we were lovers.

Here is the scene. You can put it in the present, even though it took place ten years ago, because nothing that matters to the story depends on when it took place, and you can put it in Concord, New Hampshire, even though that is indeed where it took place, because it doesn't matter where it took place, so it might as well be Concord, New Hampshire, a place I happen to know well and can therefore describe with sufficient detail to make the story believable. Around six o'clock on a Wednesday evening in late May, a man enters a bar. The bar, a cocktail lounge at street level, with a restaurant upstairs, is decorated with hanging plants and unfinished wood paneling, butcher-block tables and captain's chairs, with a half-dozen darkened, thickly upholstered booths along one wall. Three or four men between the ages of twenty-five and thirty-five are drinking at the bar and, like the man who has just entered, wear three-piece suits and loosened neckties. They are probably lawyers, young, unmarried lawyers gossiping with their brethren over martinis so as to postpone arriving home alone at their whitewashed town-house apartments, where they will fix their evening meals in radar ranges and afterwards, while their TVs chuckle quietly in front of them, sit on their couches and do a little extra work for tomorrow. They are, for the most part, honorable, educated, hard-working, shallow and moderately unhappy young men.

Our man, call him Ronald, Ron, in most ways is like these men, except that he is unusually good-looking, and that makes him a little less unhappy than they. Ron is effortlessly attractive, a genetic wonder, tall, slender, symmetrical and clean. His flaws—a small mole on the left corner of his square, not-too-prominent chin, a slight excess of blond hair on the tops of his tanned hands, and somewhat underdeveloped buttocks—insofar as they keep him from resembling too closely a men's store mannequin, only contribute to his beauty, for he is beautiful, the way we usually think of a woman as being beautiful. And he is nice too, the consequence, perhaps, of his seeming not to know how beautiful he is, to men as well as women, to young people (even children) as well as old, to attractive people (who realize immediately that he is so much more attractive than they as not to be competitive with them) as well as unattractive people.

Ron takes a seat at the bar, unfolds the evening paper in front of him, and before he can start reading, the bartender asks to help him, calling him "Sir," even though Ron has come into this bar numerous times at this time of day, especially since his divorce last fall. Ron got divorced because, after three years of marriage, his wife chose to pursue the career that his had interrupted, that of a fashion designer, which meant that she had to live in New York City while he had to continue to live in New Hampshire, where his career got its start. They agreed to live apart until he could continue his career near New York City, but after a few months, between conjugal visits, he started sleeping with other women and she started sleeping with other men, and that was that. "No big deal," he explained to friends, who liked both Ron and his wife, even though he was slightly more beautiful than she. "We really were too young when we got married, college sweethearts. But we're still best friends," he assured them. They understood. Most of Ron's friends were divorced by then too.

Ron orders a Scotch and soda with a twist and goes back to reading his paper. When his drink comes, before he takes a sip of it, he first carefully finishes reading an article about the recent reappearance of coyotes in northern New Hampshire and Vermont. He lights a cigarette. He goes on reading. He takes a second sip of his drink. Everyone in the room—the three or four men scattered along the bar, the tall, thin bartender and several people in the booths at the back—watches him do these ordinary things.

He has got to the classified section, is perhaps searching for someone willing to come in once a week and clean his apartment, when the woman who will turn out to be Sarah Cole leaves a booth in the back and approaches him. She comes up from the side and sits next to him. She's wearing heavy tan cowboy boots and a dark brown suede cowboy hat, lumpy jeans and a yellow T-shirt that clings to her arms, breasts and round belly like the skin of a sausage. Though he will later learn that she is thirty-eight years old, she looks older by about ten years, which makes her look about twenty years older than he actually is. (It's difficult to guess accurately how old Ron is; he looks anywhere from a mature twenty-five to a youthful forty, so his actual age doesn't seem to matter.)

"It's not bad here at the bar," she says, looking around. "More light, anyhow. Whatcha readin'?" she asks brightly, planting both elbows on the bar.

Ron looks up from his paper with a slight smile on his lips, sees the face of a woman homelier than any he has ever seen or imagined before, and goes on smiling lightly. He feels himself falling into her tiny, slightly crossed, dark brown eyes, pulls himself back, and studies for a few seconds her mottled, pocked complexion, bulbous nose, loose mouth, twisted and gapped teeth and heavy but receding chin. He casts a glance over her thatch of dun-colored hair and along her neck and throat, where acne burns against gray skin, and returns to her eyes and again feels himself falling into her.

"What did you say?" he asks.

She knocks a mentholated cigarette from her pack, and Ron swiftly lights it. Blowing smoke from her large, wing-shaped nostrils, she speaks again. Her voice is thick and nasal, a chocolate-colored voice. "I asked you whatcha readin', but I can see now." She belts out a single, loud laugh. "The paper!"

Ron laughs too. "The paper! The *Concord Monitor!*" He is not hallucinating, he clearly sees what is before him and admits—no, he asserts—to himself that he is speaking to the most unattractive woman he has ever seen, a fact that fascinates him, as if instead he were speaking to the most beautiful woman he has ever seen or perhaps ever will see, so he treasures the moment, attempts to hold it as if it were a golden ball, a disproportionately heavy object which—if he does not hold it lightly, with precision and firmness—will slip from his hand and roll across the lawn to the lip of the well

and down, down to the bottom of the well, lost to him forever. It will be a memory, that's all, something to speak of
wistfully and with wonder as over the years the image fades
and comes in the end to exist only in the telling. His mind
and body waken from their sleepy self-absorption, and all his
attention focuses on the woman, Sarah Cole, her ugly face,
like a warthog's, her thick, rapid speech, her dumpy, off-
center wreck of a body. To keep this moment here before
him, he begins to ask questions of her, he buys her a drink,
he smiles, until soon it seems, even to him, that he is taking
her and her life, its vicissitudes and woe, quite seriously.

He learns her name, of course, and she volunteers the information that she spoke to him on a dare from one of the
two women still sitting in the booth behind her. She turns
on her stool and smiles brazenly, triumphantly, at her
friends, two women, also homely (though nowhere as
homely as she), and dressed, like her, in cowboy boots, hats
and jeans. One of the women, a blond with an underslung
jaw and wearing heavy eye makeup, flips a little wave at her,
and as if embarrassed, she and the other woman at the booth
turn back to their drinks and sip fiercely at straws.

Sarah returns to Ron and goes on telling him what he
wants to know, about her job at Rumford Press, about her
divorced husband, who was a bastard and stupid and "sick,"
she says, as if filling suddenly with sympathy for the man.
She tells Ron about her three children, the youngest, a girl,
in junior high school and boy-crazy, the other two, boys, in
high school and almost never at home anymore. She speaks
of her children with genuine tenderness and concern and
Ron is touched. He can see with what pleasure and pain she
speaks of her children; he watches her tiny eyes light up and
water over when he asks their names.

"You're a nice woman," he informs her.

She smiles, looks at her empty glass. "No. No, I'm not. But
you're a nice man, to tell me that."

Ron, with a gesture, asks the bartender to refill Sarah's

glass. She is drinking white Russians. Perhaps she has been drinking them for an hour or two, for she seems very relaxed, more relaxed than women usually do when they come up and without introduction or invitation speak to Ron.

She asks him about himself, his job, his divorce, how long he has lived in Concord, but he finds that he is not at all interested in telling her about himself. He wants to know about her, even though what she has to tell him about herself is predictable and ordinary and the way she tells it unadorned and clichéd. He wonders about her husband. What kind of man would fall in love with Sarah Cole?

2

That scene, at Osgood's Lounge in Concord, ended with Ron's departure, alone, after having bought Sarah a second drink, and Sarah's return to her friends in the booth. I don't know what she told them, but it's not hard to imagine. The three women were not close friends, merely fellow workers at Rumford Press, where they stood at the end of a long conveyor belt day after day packing *TV Guides* into cartons. They all hated their jobs, and frequently after work, when they worked the day shift, they would put on their cowboy hats and boots, which they kept all day in their lockers, and stop for a drink or two on their way home. This had been their first visit to Osgood's, however, a place that, prior to this, they had avoided out of a sneering belief that no one went there but lawyers and insurance men. It had been Sarah who had asked the others why that should keep them away, and when they had no answer for her, the three had decided to stop at Osgood's. Ron was right, they had been there over an hour when he came in, and Sarah was a little drunk. "We'll hafta come in here again," she said to her friends, her voice rising slightly.

Which they did, that Friday, and once again Ron appeared with his evening newspaper. He put his briefcase down next to his stool and ordered a drink and proceeded to read the front page, slowly, deliberately, clearly a weary, unhurried, solitary man. He did not notice the three women in cowboy hats and boots in the booth in back, but they saw him, and after a few minutes Sarah was once again at his side.

"Hi."

He turned, saw her, and instantly regained the moment he had lost when, two nights ago, once outside the bar and on his way home, he had forgotten about the ugliest woman he had ever seen. She seemed even more grotesque to him now than before, which made the moment all the more precious to him, and so once again he held the moment as if in his hands and began to speak with her, to ask questions, to offer his opinions and solicit hers.

I said earlier that I am the man in this story and my friend Sarah Cole, now dead, is the woman. I think back to that night, the second time I had seen Sarah, and I tremble, not with fear but in shame. My concern then, when I was first becoming involved with Sarah, was merely with the moment, holding on to it, grasping it wholly, as if its beginning did not grow out of some other prior moment in her life and my life separately and at the same time did not lead into future moments in our separate lives. She talked more easily than she had the night before, and I listened as eagerly and carefully as I had before, again with the same motives, to keep her in front of me, to draw her forward from the context of her life and place her, as if she were an object, into the context of mine. I did not know how cruel this was. When you have never done a thing before and that thing is not simply and clearly right or wrong, you frequently do not know if it is a cruel thing, you just go ahead and do it and maybe later you'll be able to determine whether you acted cruelly. That way you'll know if it was right or wrong of you to have done it in the first place; too late, of course, but at least you'll know.

While we drank, Sarah told me that she hated her ex-husband because of the way he treated the children. "It's not so much the money," she said, nervously wagging her booted feet from her perch on the high barstool. "I mean, I get by, barely, but I get them fed and clothed on my own okay. It's because he won't even write them a letter or anything. He won't call them on the phone, all he calls for is to bitch at me because I'm trying to get the state to take him to court so I can get some of the money he's s'posed to be paying for child support. And he won't even think to talk to the kids when he calls. Won't even ask about them."

"He sounds like a sonofabitch."

"He is, he is!" she said. "I don't know why I married him. Or stayed married. Fourteen years, for Christ's sake. He put a spell over me or something. I don't know," she said, with a note of wistfulness in her voice. "He wasn't what you'd call good-looking."

After her second drink, she decided she had to leave. Her children were at home, it was Friday night and she liked to make sure she ate supper with them and knew where they were going and who they were with when they went out on their dates. "No dates on school nights," she said to me. "I mean, you gotta have rules, you know."

I agreed, and we left together, everyone in the place following us with his or her gaze. I was aware of that, I knew what they were thinking, and I didn't care, because I was simply walking her to her car.

It was a cool evening, dusk settling onto the lot like a gray blanket. Her car, a huge, dark green Buick sedan at least ten years old, was battered almost beyond use. She reached for the door handle on the driver's side and yanked. Nothing. The door wouldn't open. She tried again. Then I tried. Still nothing.

Then I saw it, a V-shaped dent in the left front fender, binding the metal of the door against the metal of the fender in a large crimp that held the door fast. "Someone must've backed into you while you were inside," I said to her.

She came forward and studied the crimp for a few seconds, and when she looked back at me, she was weeping. "Jesus, Jesus, Jesus!" she wailed, her large, froglike mouth wide open and wet with spit, her red tongue flopping loosely over gapped teeth. "I can't pay for this! I *can't!*" Her face was red, and even in the dusky light I could see it puff out with weeping, her tiny eyes seeming almost to disappear behind wet cheeks. Her shoulders slumped, and her hands fell limply to her sides.

Placing my briefcase on the ground, I reached out to her and put my arms around her body and held her close to me, while she cried wetly into my shoulder. After a few seconds, she started pulling herself back together and her weeping got reduced to snuffling. Her cowboy hat had been pushed back and now clung to her head at a precarious, absurdly jaunty angle. She took a step away from me and said, "I'll get in the other side."

"Okay," I said, almost in a whisper. "That's fine."

Slowly, she walked around the front of the huge, ugly vehicle and opened the door on the passenger's side and slid awkwardly across the seat until she had positioned herself behind the steering wheel. Then she started the motor, which came to life with a roar. The muffler was shot. Without saying another word to me or even waving, she dropped the car into reverse gear and backed it loudly out of the parking space and headed out of the lot to the street.

I turned and started for my car, when I happened to glance toward the door of the bar, and there, staring after me, were the bartender, the two women who had come in with Sarah, and two of the men who had been sitting at the bar. They were lawyers, and I knew them slightly. They were grinning at me. I grinned back and got into my car, and then, without looking at them again, I left the place and drove straight to my apartment.

3

One night several weeks later, Ron meets Sarah at Osgood's, and after buying her three white Russians and drinking three Scotches himself, he takes her back to his apartment in his car—a Datsun fastback coupe that she says she admires—for the sole purpose of making love to her.

I'm still the man in this story, and Sarah is still the woman, but I'm telling it this way because what I have to tell you now confuses me, embarrasses me and makes me sad, and consequently I'm likely to tell it falsely. I'm likely to cover the truth by making Sarah a better woman than she actually was, while making me appear worse than I actually was or am; or else I'll do the opposite, make Sarah worse than she was and me better. The truth is, I was pretty, extremely so, and she was not, extremely so, and I knew it and she knew it. She walked out the door of Osgood's determined to make love to a man much prettier than any she had seen up close before, and I walked out determined to make love to a woman much homelier than any I had made love to before. We were, in a sense, equals.

No, that's not exactly true. (You see? This is why I have to tell the story the way I'm telling it.) I'm not at all sure she feels as Ron does. That is to say, perhaps she genuinely likes the man, in spite of his being the most physically attractive man she has ever known. Perhaps she is more aware of her homeliness than of his beauty, for Ron, despite what I may have implied, does not think of himself as especially beautiful. He merely knows that other people think of him that way. As I said before, he is a nice man.

Ron unlocks the door to his apartment, walks in ahead of her and flicks on the lamp beside the couch. It's a small, single-bedroom, modern apartment, one of thirty identical apartments in a large brick building on the Heights just east of downtown Concord. Sarah stands nervously at the door, peering in.

"Come in, come in," Ron says.

She steps timidly in and closes the door behind her. She removes her cowboy hat, then quickly puts it back on, crosses the living room and plops down in a blond easy chair, seeming to shrink in its hug out of sight to safety. Behind her, Ron, at the entry to the kitchen, places one hand on her shoulder, and she stiffens. He removes his hand.

"Would you like a drink?"

"No . . . I guess not," she says, staring straight ahead at the wall opposite, where a large framed photograph of a bicyclist advertises in French the Tour de France. Around a corner, in an alcove off the living room, a silver-gray ten-speed bicycle leans casually against the wall, glistening and poised, slender as a thoroughbred racehorse.

"I don't know," she says. Ron is in the kitchen now, making himself a drink. "I don't know . . . I don't know."

"What? Change your mind? I can make a white Russian for you. Vodka, cream, Kahlua and ice, right?"

Sarah tries to cross her legs, but she is sitting too low in the chair and her legs are too thick at the thigh, so she ends, after a struggle, with one leg in the air and the other twisted on its side. She looks as if she has fallen from a great height.

Ron steps out from the kitchen, peers over the back of the chair, and watches her untangle herself, then ducks back into the kitchen. After a few seconds, he returns. "Seriously. Want me to fix you a white Russian?"

"No."

Ron, again from behind and above her, places one hand on Sarah's shoulder, and this time she does not stiffen, though she does not exactly relax, either. She sits there, a block of wood, staring straight ahead.

"Are you scared?" he asks gently. Then he adds, "*I* am."

"Well, no. I'm not scared." She remains silent for a mo-

ment. "You're scared? Of what?" She turns to face him but
avoids his blue eyes.

"Well . . . I don't do this all the time, you know. Bring
home a woman I . . . ," he trails off.

"Picked up in a bar."

"No. I mean, I like you, Sarah. I really do. And I didn't
just pick you up in a bar, you know that. We've gotten to be
friends, you and me."

"You want to sleep with me?" she asks, still not meeting
his steady gaze.

"Yes." He seems to mean it. He does not take a gulp or
even a sip from his drink. He just says, "Yes," straight out,
and cleanly, not too quickly, either, and not after a hesitant
delay. A simple statement of a simple fact. The man wants
to make love to the woman. She asked him, and he told her.
What could be simpler?

"Do you want to sleep with *me?*" he asks.

She turns around in the chair, faces the wall again, and
says in a low voice, "Sure I do, but . . . it's hard to explain."

"What? But what?" Placing his glass down on the table
between the chair and the sofa, he puts both hands on her
shoulders and lightly kneads them. He knows he can be dis-
couraged from pursuing this, but he is not sure how easily.
Having got this far without bumping against obstacles (except the ones he has placed in his way himself), he is not sure
what it will take to turn him back. He does not know, therefore, how assertive or how seductive he should be with her.
He suspects that he can be stopped very easily, so he is reluc-
tant to give her a chance to try. He goes on kneading her
doughy shoulders.

"You and me . . . we're real different." She glances at the
bicycle in the corner.

"A man . . . and a woman," he says.

"No, not that. I mean, different. That's all. Real different.
More than you . . . You're nice, but you don't know what I

mean, and that's one of the things that makes you so nice. But we're different. Listen," she says, "I gotta go. I gotta leave now."

The man removes his hands and retrieves his glass, takes a sip and watches her over the rim of the glass, as, not without difficulty, the woman rises from the chair and moves swiftly toward the door. She stops at the door, squares her hat on her head, and glances back at him.

"We can be friends, okay?"

"Okay. Friends."

"I'll see you again down at Osgood's, right?"

"Oh, yeah, sure."

"Good. See you," she says, opening the door.

The door closes. The man walks around the sofa, snaps on the television set, and sits down in front of it. He picks up a *TV Guide* from the coffee table and flips through it, stops, runs a finger down the listings, stops, puts down the magazine and changes the channel. He does not once connect the magazine in his hand to the woman who has just left his apartment, even though he knows she spends her days packing *TV Guide*s into cartons that get shipped to warehouses in distant parts of New England. He'll think of the connection some other night, but by then the connection will be merely sentimental. It'll be too late for him to understand what she meant by "different."

4

But that's not the point of my story. Certainly, it's an aspect of the story, the political aspect, if you want, but it's not the reason I'm trying to tell the story in the first place. I'm trying to tell the story so that I can understand what happened between me and Sarah Cole that summer and early autumn ten years ago. To say we were lovers says very little about what happened; to say we were friends says even less. No, if I'm to understand the whole thing, I'll have to say the whole thing, for, in the end, what I need to know is whether what happened between me and Sarah Cole was right or wrong. Character is fate, which suggests that if a man can know and then to some degree control his character, he can know and to that same degree control his fate.

But let me go on with my story. The next time Sarah and I were together we were at her apartment in the south end of Concord, a second-floor flat in a tenement building on Perley Street. I had stayed away from Osgood's for several weeks, deliberately trying to avoid running into Sarah there, though I never quite put it that way to myself. I found excuses and generated interest in and reasons for going elsewhere after work. Yet I was obsessed with Sarah by then, obsessed with the idea of making love to her, which, because it was not an actual *desire* to make love to her, was an unusually complex obsession. Passion without desire, if it gets expressed, may in fact be a kind of rape, and perhaps I sensed the danger that lay behind my obsession and for that reason went out of my way to avoid meeting Sarah again.

Yet I did meet her, inadvertently, of course. After picking up shirts at the cleaner's on South Main and Perley streets, I'd gone down Perley on my way to South State and the post office. It was a Saturday morning, and this trip on my bicycle was part of my regular Saturday routine. I did not remember that Sarah lived on Perley Street, although she had told me several times in a complaining way—it's a rough neighborhood, packed-dirt yards, shabby apartment buildings, the carcasses of old, half-stripped cars on cinder blocks in the driveways, broken red and yellow plastic tricycles on the cracked sidewalks—but as soon as I saw her, I remembered. It was too late to avoid meeting her. I was riding my bike, wearing shorts and T-shirt, the package containing my folded and starched shirts hooked to the carrier behind me, and she was walking toward me along the sidewalk, lugging two large bags of groceries. She saw me, and I stopped. We talked, and I offered to carry her groceries for her. I took the bags while she led the bike, handling it carefully, as if she were afraid she might break it.

At the stoop we came to a halt. The wooden steps were cluttered with half-opened garbage bags spilling eggshells, coffee grounds and old food wrappers to the walkway. "I can't get the people downstairs to take care of their garbage," she explained. She leaned the bike against the banister and reached for her groceries.

"I'll carry them up for you," I said. I directed her to loop the chain lock from the bike to the banister rail and snap it shut and told her to bring my shirts up with her.

"Maybe you'd like a beer?" she said as she opened the door to the darkened hallway. Narrow stairs disappeared in front of me into heavy, damp darkness, and the air smelled like old newspapers.

"Sure," I said, and followed her up.

"Sorry there's no light. I can't get them to fix it."

"No matter. I can see you and follow along," I said, and even in the dim light of the hall I could see the large, dark blue veins that cascaded thickly down the backs of her legs. She wore tight, white-duck Bermuda shorts, rubber shower sandals and a pink sleeveless sweater. I pictured her in the cashier's line at the supermarket. I would have been behind her, a stranger, and on seeing her, I would have turned away and studied the covers of the magazines, *TV Guide*, *People*, the *National Enquirer*, for there was nothing of interest in her appearance that in the hard light of day would not have slightly embarrassed me. Yet here I was inviting myself into her home, eagerly staring at the backs of her ravaged legs, her sad, tasteless clothing, her poverty. I was not detached, however, was not staring at her with scientific curiosity, and because of my passion, did not feel or believe that what I was doing was perverse. I felt warmed by her presence and was flirtatious and bold, a little pushy, even.

Picture this. The man, tanned, limber, wearing red jogging shorts, Italian leather sandals, a clinging net T-shirt of

Scandinavian design and manufacture, enters the apartment behind the woman, whose dough-colored skin, thick, short body and homely, uncomfortable face all try, but fail, to hide themselves. She waves him toward the table in the kitchen, where he sets down the bags and looks good-naturedly around the room. "What about the beer you bribed me with?" he asks.

The apartment is dark and cluttered with old, oversized furniture, yard sale and secondhand stuff bought originally for a large house in the country or a spacious apartment on a boulevard forty or fifty years ago, passed down from antique dealer to used-furniture store to yard sale to thrift shop, where it finally gets purchased by Sarah Cole and gets hauled over to Perley Street and shoved up the narrow stairs, she and her children grunting and sweating in the darkness of the hallway—overstuffed armchairs and couch, huge, ungainly dressers, upholstered rocking chairs, and in the kitchen, an old flat-topped maple desk for a table, a half-dozen heavy oak dining room chairs, a high, glass-fronted cabinet, all peeling, stained, chipped and squatting heavily on a dark green linoleum floor.

The place is neat and arranged in a more or less orderly way, however, and the man seems comfortable there. He strolls from the kitchen to the living room and peeks into the three small bedrooms that branch off a hallway behind the living room. "Nice place!" he calls to the woman. He is studying the framed pictures of her three children arranged as if on an altar atop the buffet. "Nice-looking kids!" he calls out. They are. Blond, round-faced, clean and utterly ordinary-looking, their pleasant faces glance, as instructed, slightly off camera and down to the right, as if they are trying to remember the name of the capital of Montana.

When he returns to the kitchen, the woman is putting away her groceries, her back to him. "Where's that beer you bribed me with?" he asks again. He takes a position against the doorframe, his weight on one hip, like a dancer resting.

"You sure are quiet today, Sarah," he says in a low voice. "Everything okay?"

Silently, she turns away from the grocery bags, crosses the room to the man, reaches up to him, and holding him by the head, kisses his mouth, rolls her torso against his, drops her hands to his hips and yanks him tightly to her and goes on kissing him, eyes closed, working her face furiously against his. The man places his hands on her shoulders and pulls away, and they face each other, wide-eyed, as if amazed and frightened. The man drops his hands, and the woman lets go of his hips. Then, after a few seconds, the man silently turns, goes to the door, and leaves. The last thing he sees as he closes the door behind him is the woman standing in the kitchen doorframe, her face looking down and slightly to one side, wearing the same pleasant expression on her face as her children in their photographs, trying to remember the capital of Montana.

5

Sarah appeared at my apartment door the following morning, a Sunday, cool and rainy. She had brought me the package of freshly laundered shirts I'd left in her kitchen, and when I opened the door to her, she simply held the package out to me, as if it were a penitent's gift. She wore a yellow rain slicker and cap and looked more like a disconsolate schoolgirl facing an angry teacher than a grown woman dropping a package off at a friend's apartment. After all, she had nothing to be ashamed of.

I invited her inside, and she accepted my invitation. I had been reading the Sunday *New York Times* on the couch and drinking coffee, lounging through the gray morning in bathrobe and pajamas. I told her to take off her wet raincoat and hat and hang them in the closet by the door and started for the kitchen to get her a cup of coffee, when I stopped, turned and looked at her. She closed the closet door on her yellow raincoat and hat, turned around and faced me.

What else can I do? I must describe it. I remember that moment of ten years ago as if it occurred ten minutes ago, the package of shirts on the table behind her, the newspapers scattered over the couch and floor, the sound of wind-blown rain washing the side of the building outside and the silence of the room, as we stood across from one another and watched, while we each simultaneously removed our own clothing, my robe, her blouse and skirt, my pajama top, her slip and bra, my pajama bottom, her underpants, until we were both standing naked in the harsh gray light, two naked members of the same species, a male and a female, the male somewhat younger and less scarred than the female, the female somewhat less delicately constructed than the male, both individuals pale-skinned, with dark thatches of hair in the area of their genitals, both individuals standing slackly, as if a great, protracted tension between them had at last been released.

6

We made love that morning in my bed for long hours that drifted easily into afternoon. And we talked, as people usually do when they spend half a day or half a night in bed together. I told her of my past, named and described the people whom I had loved and had loved me, my ex-wife in New York, my brother in the air force, my mother in San Diego, and I told her of my ambitions and dreams and even confessed some of my fears. She listened patiently and intelligently throughout and talked much less than I. She had already told me many of these things about herself, and perhaps whatever she had to say to me now lay on the next inner circle of intimacy or else could not be spoken of at all.

During the next few weeks, we met and made love often, and always at my apartment. On arriving home from work, I would phone her, or if not, she would phone me, and after a few feints and dodges, one would suggest to the other that we get together tonight, and a half hour later she'd be at my

door. Our lovemaking was passionate, skillful, kindly and
deeply satisfying. We didn't often speak of it to one another
or brag about it, the way some couples do when they are surprised by the ease with which they have become contented
lovers. We did occasionally joke and tease each other, however, playfully acknowledging that the only thing we did together was make love but that we did it so frequently there
was no time for anything else.

Then one hot night, a Saturday in August, we were lying
in bed atop the tangled sheets, smoking cigarettes and chat-
ting idly, and Sarah suggested that we go out for a drink.

"Out? Now?"

"Sure. It's early. What time is it?"

I scanned the digital clock next to the bed. "Nine forty-
nine."

"There. See?"

"That's not so early. You usually go home by eleven, you
know. It's almost ten."

"No, it's only a little after nine. Depends on how you look
at things. Besides, Ron, it's Saturday night. Don't you want
to go out and dance or something? Or is this the only thing
you know how to do?" she said, and poked me in the ribs.
"You know how to dance? You like to dance?"

"Yeah, sure . . . sure, but not tonight. It's too hot. And I'm
tired."

But she persisted, happily pointing out that an air-
conditioned bar would be as cool as my apartment, and we
didn't have to go to a dance bar, we could go to Osgood's.
"As a compromise," she said.

I suggested a place called the El Rancho, a restaurant
with a large, dark cocktail lounge and dance bar located several miles from town on the old Portsmouth highway.
Around nine the restaurant closed and the bar became
something of a roadhouse, with a small country-and-western
band and a clientele drawn from the four or five villages that
adjoined Concord on the north and east. I had eaten at the

restaurant once but had never gone to the bar, and I didn't know anyone who had.

Sarah was silent for a moment. Then she lighted a cigarette and drew the sheet over her naked body. "You don't want anybody to know about us, do you? Do you?"

"That's not it. . . . I just don't like gossip, and I work with a lot of people who show up sometimes at Osgood's. On a Saturday night especially."

"No," she said firmly. "You're ashamed of being seen with me. You'll sleep with me, all right, but you won't go out in public with me."

"That's not true, Sarah."

She was silent again. Relieved, I reached across her to the bed table and got my cigarettes and lighter.

"You owe me, Ron," she said suddenly, as I passed over her. "You owe me."

"What?" I lay back, lighted a cigarette, and covered my body with the sheet.

"I said, 'You owe me.' "

"I don't know what you're talking about, Sarah. I just don't like a lot of gossip going around, that's all. I like keeping my private life private, that's all. I don't *owe* you anything."

"Friendship you owe me. And respect. Friendship and respect. A person can't do what you've done with me without owing them friendship and respect."

"Sarah, I really don't know what you're talking about," I said. "I am your friend, you know that. And I respect you. I do."

"You really think so, don't you?"

"Yes. Of course."

She said nothing for several long moments. Then she sighed and in a low, almost inaudible voice said, "Then you'll have to go out in public with me. I don't care about Osgood's or the people you work with, we don't have to go there or see any of them," she said. "But you're gonna have to go to places like the El Rancho with me, and a few other places I know, too, where there's people *I* know, people *I* work with, and maybe we'll even go to a couple of parties, because *I* get invited to parties sometimes, you know. I have friends, and I have some family, too, and you're gonna have to meet my family. My kids think I'm just going around barhopping when I'm over here with you, and I don't like that, so you're gonna have to meet them so I can tell them where I am when I'm not at home nights. And sometimes you're gonna come over and spend the evening at my place!" Her voice had risen as she heard her demands and felt their rightness, until now she was almost shouting at me. "You *owe* that to me. Or else you're a bad man. It's that simple, Ron."

It was.

7

The handsome man is overdressed. He is wearing a navy blue blazer, taupe shirt open at the throat, white slacks, white loafers. Everyone else, including the homely woman with the handsome man, is dressed appropriately—that is, like everyone else—jeans and cowboy boots, blouses or cowboy shirts or T-shirts with catchy sayings or the names of country-and-western singers printed across the front, and many of the women are wearing cowboy hats pushed back and tied under their chins.

The man doesn't know anyone at the bar or, if they're at a party, in the room, but the woman knows most of the people there, and she gladly introduces him. The men grin and shake his hand, slap him on his jacketed shoulder, ask him where he works, what's his line, after which they lapse into silence. The women flirt briefly with their faces, but they lapse into silence even before the men do. The woman with the man in the blazer does most of the talking for everyone. She talks for the man in the blazer, for the men standing around the refrigerator, or if they're at a bar, for the other men at the table, and for the other women too. She chats and rambles aimlessly through loud monologues, laughs uproariously at trivial jokes and drinks too much, until soon she is drunk, thick-tongued, clumsy, and the man has to say her goodbyes and ease her out the door to his car and drive her home to her apartment on Perley Street.

This happens twice in one week and then three times the next—at the El Rancho, at the Ox Bow in Northwood, at Rita and Jimmy's apartment on Thorndike Street, out in Warner at Betsy Beeler's new house and, the last time, at a cottage on Lake Sunapee rented by some kids in shipping at Rumford Press. Ron no longer calls Sarah when he gets home from work; he waits for her call, and sometimes, when he knows it's she, he doesn't answer the phone. Usually, he lets it ring five or six times, and then he reaches down and picks up the receiver. He has taken his jacket and vest off and loosened his tie and is about to put his supper, frozen manicotti, into the radar range.

"Hello?"

"Hi."

"How're you doing?"

"Okay, I guess. A little tired."

"Still hung over?"

"Naw. Not really. Just tired. I hate Mondays."

"You have fun last night?"

"Well, yeah, sorta. It's nice out there, at the lake. Listen," she says, brightening. "Whyn't you come over here tonight? The kids're all going out later, but if you come over before eight, you can meet them. They really want to meet you."

"You told them about me?"

"Sure. Long time ago. I'm not supposed to tell my own kids?"

Ron is silent.

She says, "You don't want to come over here tonight. You don't want to meet my kids. No, you don't want my kids to meet *you*, that's it."

"No, no, it's just . . . I've got a lot of work to do. . . ."

"We should talk," she announces in a flat voice.

"Yes," he says. "We should talk."

They agree that she will meet him at his apartment, and they'll talk, and they say goodbye and hang up.

While Ron is heating his supper and then eating it alone at his kitchen table and Sarah is feeding her children, perhaps I should admit, since we are nearing the end of my story, that I don't actually know that Sarah Cole is dead. A few years ago I happened to run into one of her friends from the press, a blond woman with an underslung jaw. Her name, she reminded me, was Glenda; she had seen me at Osgood's a couple of times and we had met at the El Rancho once when I had gone there with Sarah. I was amazed that she could remember me and a little embarrassed that I did not recognize her at all, and she laughed at that and said, "You haven't changed much, mister!" I pretended to recognize her then, but I think she knew she was a stranger to me. We were standing outside the Sears store on South Main Street, where I had gone to buy paint. I had recently remarried, and my wife and I were redecorating my apartment.

"Whatever happened to Sarah?" I asked Glenda. "Is she still down at the press?"

"Jeez, no! She left a long time ago. Way back. I heard she went back with her ex-husband. I can't remember his name, something Cole. Eddie Cole, maybe."

I asked her if she was sure of that, and she said no, she had only heard it around the bars and down at the press, but she had assumed it was true. People said Sarah had moved back with her ex-husband and was living for a while with him and the kids in a trailer in a park near Hooksett, and then when the kids, or at least the boys, got out of school, the rest of them moved down to Florida or someplace because he was out of work. He was a carpenter, she thought.

"He was mean to her," I said. "I thought he used to beat her up and everything. I thought she hated him."

"Oh, well, yeah, he was a bastard, all right. I met him a couple times, and I didn't like him. Short, ugly and mean when he got drunk. But you know what they say."

"What do they say?"

"Oh, you know, about water seeking its own level and all."

"Sarah wasn't mean when she was drunk."

The woman laughed. "Naw, but she sure was short and ugly!"

I said nothing.

"Hey, don't get me wrong," Glenda said. "I liked Sarah. But you and her . . . well, you sure made a funny-looking couple. She probably didn't feel so self-conscious and all with her husband," she said somberly. "I mean, with you, all tall and blond, and poor old Sarah . . . I mean, the way them kids in the press room used to kid her about her looks, it was embarrassing just to have to hear it."

"Well . . . I loved her," I said.

The woman raised her plucked eyebrow in disbelief. She smiled. "Sure, you did, honey," she said, and she patted me on the arm. "Sure, you did." Then she let the smile drift off her face, turned and walked away from me.

When someone you have loved dies, you accept the fact of his or her death, but then the person goes on living in your memory, dreams and reveries. You have imaginary conversations with him or her, you see something striking and remind yourself to tell your loved one about it and then get brought up short by the knowledge of the fact of his or her death, and at night, in your sleep, the dead person visits you. With Sarah, none of that happened. When she was gone from my life, she was gone absolutely, as if she had never existed in the first place. It was only later, when I could think of her as dead and could come out and say it, my friend Sarah Cole is dead, that I was able to tell this story, for that is when she began to enter my memories, my dreams and my reveries. In that way, I learned that I truly did love her, and now

I have begun to grieve over her death, to wish her alive again, so that I can say to her the things I could not know or say when she was alive, when I did not know that I loved her.

8

The woman arrives at Ron's apartment around eight. He hears her car, because of the broken muffler, blat and rumble into the parking lot below, and he crosses quickly from the kitchen and peers out the living room window and, as if through a telescope, watches her shove herself across the seat to the passenger's side to get out of the car, then walk slowly in the dusky light toward the apartment building. It's a warm evening, and she's wearing her white Bermuda shorts, pink sleeveless sweater and shower sandals. Ron hates those clothes. He hates the way the shorts cut into her flesh at the crotch and thigh, hates the large, dark caves below her arms that get exposed by the sweater, hates the sucking noise made by the sandals.

Shortly, there is a soft knock at his door. He opens it, turns away and crosses to the kitchen, where he turns back, lights a cigarette and watches her. She closes the door. He offers her a drink, which she declines, and somewhat formally, he invites her to sit down. She sits carefully on the sofa, in the middle, with her feet close together on the floor, as if she were being interviewed for a job. Then he comes around and sits in the easy chair, relaxed, one leg slung over the other at the knee, as if he were interviewing her for the job.

"Well," he says, "you wanted to talk."

"Yes. But now you're mad at me. I can see that. I didn't do anything, Ron."

"I'm not mad at you."

They are silent for a moment. Ron goes on smoking his cigarette.

Finally, she sighs and says, "You don't want to see me anymore, do you?"

He waits a few seconds and answers, "Yes. That's right." Getting up from the chair, he walks to the silver-gray bicycle and stands before it, running a fingertip along the slender crossbar from the saddle to the chrome-plated handlebars.

"You're a sonofabitch," she says in a low voice. "You're worse than my ex-husband." Then she smiles meanly, almost sneers, and soon he realizes that she is telling him that she won't leave. He's stuck with her, she informs him with cold precision. "You think I'm just so much meat, and all you got to do is call up the butcher shop and cancel your order. Well, now you're going to find out different. You *can't* cancel your order. I'm not meat, I'm not one of your pretty little girlfriends who come running when you want them and go away when you get tired of them. I'm *different!* I got nothing to lose, Ron. Nothing. So you're stuck with me, Ron."

He continues stroking his bicycle. "No, I'm not."

She sits back in the couch and crosses her legs at the ankles. "I think I *will* have that drink you offered."

"Look, Sarah, it would be better if you go now."

"No," she says flatly. "You offered me a drink when I came in. Nothing's changed since I've been here. Not for me and not for you. I'd like that drink you offered," she says haughtily.

Ron turns away from the bicycle and takes a step toward her. His face has stiffened into a mask. "Enough is enough," he says through clenched teeth. "I've given you enough."

"Fix me a drink, will you, honey?" she says with a phony smile.

Ron orders her to leave.

She refuses.

He grabs her by the arm and yanks her to her feet.

She starts crying lightly. She stands there and looks up into his face and weeps, but she does not move toward the door, so he pushes her. She regains her balance and goes on weeping.

He stands back and places his fists on his hips and looks at her. "Go on, go on and leave, you ugly bitch," he says to her, and as he says the words, as one by one they leave his mouth, she's transformed into the most beautiful woman he has ever seen. He says the words again, almost tenderly. "Leave, you ugly bitch." Her hair is golden, her brown eyes deep and sad, her mouth full and affectionate, her tears the tears of love and loss, and her pleading, outstretched arms, her entire body, the arms and body of a devoted woman's cruelly rejected love. A third time he says the words. "Leave me now, you disgusting, ugly bitch." She is wrapped in an envelope of golden light, a warm, dense haze that she seems to have stepped into, as into a carriage. And then she is gone, and he is alone again.

He looks around the room, as if searching for her. Sitting down in the easy chair, he places his face in his hands. It's not as if she has died; it's as if he has killed her.

Captions

———•————⟨⟨

1

Raising glassfuls of "home brew," Early and Dora Keep, the proud parents of the bride, toast the grateful parents of the groom, Roger ("Rog") and Estelle LaBas. Early is Catamount's trusted game warden, and Rog, proprietor of LaBas Hardware Co., is fondly remembered for his hilarious portrayal of the German shepherd in the Suncook Players' production last fall of the famous German comedy play, *Dog Food.* Their wives, Dora and Estelle, have long been active in community bake sales and bean suppers. This wedding joins not only two of Catamount High School's favorite members of the class of 1984, but two of our town's most popular families as well. Congratulations to all the Keeps and all the LaBases too! Congratula

2

In the background, next to the refrigerator, Charles ("Chuck") LaBas, the lucky groom, and Swenda Keep, now the lovely Mrs. LaBas, are about to cut their beautiful wedding cake, made and presented to the happy couple by the students of the Suncook Valley Cake Decorating School. Chuck played goalie for last year's Catamount High championship hockey team and is now employed as a line repairman for the Public Service Co. Swenda was the valedictorian of her 1984 class at CHS and since graduation has been a student at the Suncook Valley Cake Decorating School. After their wedding trip to Maine, the happy couple plans to live in their new mobile home on Blake's Hill Ro

3

After five heartless days of cold rain, at last the sun appears, and Swenda lies on the beach at Ogunquit picking up the tan she knows her friends at home expect to see and talk about when she returns, so they won't have to talk even obliquely about the "wedding night," which would embarrass the girls, who all know that she is now ten weeks pregnant and has been "doing it" with Chuck in his Tempest since Christmas Eve, which really didn't bother anyone then but now for reasons Swenda can't understand embarrasses everyone who knows she is pregnant and had to

4

After another night at the hotel bar talking to the hookers, Chuck wakes and his hangover glues his body to the bed, while Swenda, on the beach since

5

In the breakfast nook of their mobile home, Chuck is patiently explaining to Swenda: "It's the only rational thing to do, now that you've had the miscarriage and we can finally be honest with each other and ourselves. We were too young, that's all, and now that you're not pregnant anymore, we can decide freely if we want to stay married, and honestly, honey, of course I still love you, that's not the question, because I wouldn't have asked you to marry me if I hadn't thought you were pregnant and all. Besides, we're still young and have our whole lives before us, like they say, though I'm not saying we should get a divorce or anything, you understand, but maybe if I *was* in the air force for four years, when I got out we'd know for sure if we wanted to stay married or not, and in the meantime you can live here in the trailer and have my support check from the air force and whatever you make off your cake decorating and, you know, we could find out about ourselves a little more, and that way we could be sure of how we felt towards each other without being forced int

6

"Oh my Christ, my good God, my sweet Jesus Christ, I don't know what we're going to do now! It's all over, all gone, everything's turned to *shit!*" Swenda wails, as Chuck grimly, silently, kicks at the blackened wreckage of their home. (The intensity of the fire melted the refrigerator of the mobile home of Charles and Swenda LaBas, shown at right with refrigerator. The LaBases are recent newlyweds who had lived here for only two

7

months ago, seen here cheerfully posing at the door of the "Chalet" model mobile home minutes after it had been delivered by the Bide-a-Wile Home Corp., remember, honey?

8

"How could things get so complicated so fast? I feel old."

"I thought it would be easy to love me. I thought the hard part would be loving you. It would have been simple if I had been all right or else all wrong. I feel old, too."

9

We'll be all right together.
I'll be head repairman in a year.
My father's a happy man and
your father is, too, aren't they?
My mother is a happy woman, too,
and your mother's a good cook.
Many things make many people
happy, why not the two of us?
So this is life. Oh Jesus.
We'll be all right together.
I want to have a baby, Chuck.
I hope he looks like you did.
I hope he looks like *you* did.
I want you to have my baby.
This time it'll mean something.
We'll just save our pennies.
I'll try out for the Players.
I'll be head repairman in a year.
We'll be as happy as we can be.
America is a wonderful place
to be young and in love with love.
We were kids. Now we're grownups, so
this time it'll mean something.
I don't understand the darkness
that seemed to surround us then.
I'll be head repairman in a year.
I'm glad I didn't join the air force.
Your cakes are the talk of the town.
So this is a happy marriage.
We'll be all right together, you,

me and the baby, a family now.
My cakes are the talk of the town.
I'm glad you didn't join the air force.
So this is life. It's not bad.
I still wonder about the darkness
that seemed to surround us then.
We were kids then. Now we're grownups.
Now we've got kids of our own, and
here they are. The one on the right

Firewood

Nelson Painter is a man who is old but doesn't know it yet. The calendars, the clocks, the dates and names of events he remembers and, though they're private and not that reliable on their own, his memories themselves—they all tell him he's not an old man, not yet, not this early in the game. Everything but his body tells him it's impossible to come up only sixty-one and old, and even his body's ambiguous about it, because it's impossible, for instance, for a truly old man to be out of bed as he is every morning of the year at six, even on a Sunday in midwinter when it's still dark as night and snow is lightly falling and the temperature's stuck at fifteen below and he slides his slippers and bathrobe on in the dark so as not to wake the wife and moves to the bathroom to pee in a hurry and then, hands stuck in the pockets of the robe because the house is so cold, he gets quickly downstairs, with the lights on now, follows his breath down the stairs that creak a familiar tune under his feet as he descends to the living room, crosses to the door of the kitchen, unlatches the low gate, and greets with a nod the dog, stiff between her dysplastic hips, a seven-year-old Great Dane with one yellow and one brown eye.

The dog clatters its nails on the linoleum floor and waits at the door for the man to switch on the overhead light, latch back the gate to the living room, where the thick furniture and carpeting sit sanctified and permanently new, as in a department store window display, and finally open the outside door and the aluminum storm door and release the huge, lumbering dog to the yard. Nelson stands a moment behind the silvery frosted glass and tries to remember his dream of a moment ago. It was years ago, in the dream. It was like most of his dreams that way, a phenomenon that goes on disturbing him, irritating him, actually, infuriating him sometimes, because you ought to be able to move on in your dreams just as you move on in your life. Your kids grow up, you marry another woman, you move away, come back, change and change again. You'd think your dreams would know that and would somehow deal with that. He knows he's not thinking the same thoughts he thought ten and twenty years ago. Why the hell, then, is he dreaming the same dreams? Not exactly, of course, but almost—and in tone and atmosphere and most of the settings and many of the people, too, his dreams now are the same as his dreams when he was a young man of thirty and forty and his kids were kids and he was married to their mother.

His life then was loud and boisterous and quarrelsome most of the time, "a pressure cooker," he called it, but not all bad, surely not as bad as his first wife said and as he thought then, though he was not wrong to leave her and the kids and move on to another life, another woman, who doesn't fight him so hard all the time, who seems to like him better than his first wife liked him, or rather, seems to like the aspects of his character that he himself likes, or believes he likes. Or wants to like. His humor, for instance. He is funny, quick, sarcastic, in an intelligently cruel way that surprises people and makes most of them laugh. And his being so principled, which you might call an unwillingness to compromise or intolerance, if, like his first wife, who did not understand a lot of things about him, you didn't understand his belief in his own beliefs. And then there is his independence, his insistence that he needs no one's love, though he claims to be pleased by what he's given and says he has plenty of love of his own to give back. Still, at bottom, when push comes to shove, as he says, he does not *respect* love, which fact pleases him.

He can't see the snow falling, but he knows it's coming down—perhaps he can hear it, flecks of white ticking the frozen ground. When you've lived a lifetime or nearly so within fifty miles of where you were born, your body responds to shifts in weather well ahead of your mind, so that to predict the weather you consult your body and not the weather itself. As the pressure drops, one's skin tightens, one smells moisture in the air, hears snow flurries falling in the dark, and one knows what's coming. The body of Nelson Painter this early morning in mid-January in central New Hampshire knows the barometer is falling, the humidity and temperature are rising, and there is a snowstorm coming from the southwest, a blizzard maybe, and as a result Nelson knows that the cord of firewood, two-foot-long chunks of maple and birch dumped in a heap in his yard beside the driveway a month ago, will be covered in a foot or two of snow by noon, which disgusts him, because the boy should have come over and picked up the wood two or more weeks ago or even before Christmas, the day Nelson called him and told him about the wood, his Christmas present to his son. There wasn't any snow then, and the ground, frozen solid since November, was as hard as steel plate, and the wood, dumped unceremoniously from an old stake-bodied truck by the same local man who sold Nelson his winter's wood every year, ten cords of it, had bounced and rolled over the ground, a sprawl of a pile that instantly looked ugly to Nelson. But he thought his son would drive right over from Concord in his Japanese pickup and haul it home, so he left it there on the bony lawn by the driveway. Then, after Christmas there was a thaw, the "January thaw," and the yard turned to muck, the wood sank under its own weight, and it rained, and then there came a freeze again, a hard freeze, and now the wood is glued to the yard, as if molecules of maple and birch have been welded to molecules of frozen dead grass and dirt.

Nelson looks into the silver layer of frost covering the storm door before him and knows that it's lightly snowing on the other side, and he says to himself, I'll have to call the bastard and get him over here to haul away his own damn Christmas present, or else I'll have to see it there in the spring, coming up out of the melting snow like a damn bone-yard. He closes the inner door and steps away, and a moment later he's on his knees in front of his woodstove, a cast-iron Ranger from Sears, low and deep enough for two-footers. He crumples last Sunday's *Union-Leader* into balls and twists of paper, chucks sticks of kindling split off maple logs, scratches a match against the tray in front of the stove, tosses it in and clanks the door shut, and rolling back on his heels, listens to the stove sigh and moan and the flames inside begin to catch and feed and grow.

A moment later Nelson stands up slowly, shambles from the stove to the sink, reaches into the overhead cabinet on the right, next to the small square window that looks into the darkness of the backyard and field and woods beyond, and he draws out the bottle of vodka. With his other hand he reaches into the overhead cabinet on the left and plucks a juice glass from a stack and places it on the drainboard. Then, his right hand trembling only slightly, he fills the glass with vodka, recaps the bottle and places it back inside the cabinet, and now he enjoys his first drink of the day, a delib-erate, slow act as measured and radiant as a sacrament, as sweet to him as the sun rising over the winter-burnt New Hampshire hills, as clean as new frost. That first drink is the best drink of the day. It's as if all the others he will drink from now until he falls back into his bed tonight he drinks solely to make this first drink wonderful. Without them and without the need they create in his blood, this first drink would be as nothing, a mere preliminary to preliminaries. With them, it's the culmination of Nelson's day. He sips at the vodka steadily, as if nibbling at it, and his gratitude for it is nearly boundless, and though he appears to be studying the darkness out the window, he's seeing only as far as the glass in his hand and is thinking only about the vodka as it fits like a tiny, pellucid pouch into his mouth, breaks into a thin stream and rolls down his throat, warming his chest as it passes and descends into his stomach, where the alcohol enters his blood and then his heart and brain, enlarging him and bringing him to heated life, filling the stony, cold man with light and feeling and sentiment even, blessing him with an exact nostalgia for the very seconds of his life as they pass, which in this man is as close to love as he has been able to come for years, maybe since childhood.

Outside, the dog scratches feebly at the door, almost apologetically, and Nelson, after first rinsing the glass and placing it back into the cabinet, finally turns and lets the cold animal in. She's abject and seems eager to stay out of the man's way, which is difficult since both of them are large and the room is small, but when he crosses to check on the woodstove, the dog limps quickly away and stands by the sink until he returns, and then she moves back by the door, where she watches, waiting until he sets the coffeepot on the electric range and sits down at the Formica-topped table at the far wall. Finally, as Nelson unfolds yesterday's paper and begins to read, the dog circles and lies down next to the woodstove, arranging herself in an ungainly heap of legs and tail, neck, muzzle and ears, a collapsed, fawn-colored tent.

The sound an hour later of Nelson dialing the telephone wakes the dog. She lifts her heavy head and watches him at the table, dialing the phone on the wall beside him. The room is filled with white light now and smells of coffee and toasted bread and woodsmoke. Nelson holds the receiver loosely to his ear and lets it ring, eight, nine, ten times, until his son answers.

"H'lo?"

"Good morning."

"Oh, hi, Dad."

"Did I wake you up?"

"Well—yeah. It's what, eight? No, Jesus, it's not even seven-thirty. What's up?"

"You, now. Want me to call back later? You alone? You got somebody there?"

"Ha. Not very likely. Yeah, I'm alone, all right. No, no, you don't need to call back, I can talk, I'm awake. I was just up late last night, that's all," he says. Then, with great heartiness, "So—what's happening? How're you doing?"

Nelson says fine and comes right to the point of his call: "You got a cord of firewood sitting out here in my yard, Earl, and the snow's starting to fly already, so if you want to burn any of that stuff this winter, you better drive over here and get it out this morning."

Earl says damn, but quickly assures his father that he'll be over in a few hours. "Be good to see you anyhow," he adds. "I haven't seen you since what, Christmas?"

"Before."

"Right, before. Well—we got to catch up."

Nelson agrees, and the men say goodbye and hang up. Then Nelson gets stiffly up from the table and tosses a log from the woodbox into the stove, goes to the cabinet over the sink and brings down the vodka bottle and juice glass and pours his second drink of the day. The dog watches, her yellow and brown eyes drooping from the heat. Then she closes her eyes and sleeps.

The woman in Nelson Painter's dream is sometimes his first wife, Adele, who lives out in San Diego now, alone, and sometimes she's Allie, his second wife, who lives with him in this house, where as town clerk she runs her office from the room he made out of the shed that connects the house

to the barn. In the dream, it doesn't seem to matter, Adele
or Allie; they behave the same way—they scream at him, a
roar, high and windy, a frightening mix of rage and revulsion
that blames him for everything in general and nothing in
particular. The dream always takes place in New Hampshire, though sometimes it's set in the tenements and trailers
he shared with Adele when they were young and raising
their three kids, when Nelson was an apprentice and then
a journeyman carpenter, working out of the Catamount
local; and sometimes the dream is set in this house, a reno-
vated nineteenth-century farmhouse he bought when he
married Allie and started making good money running work
for the state and large out-of-state contractors building New
Hampshire dams, hospitals and now the Seabrook nuclear
power plant. Nelson is no longer running work, no longer
a foreman, of course, for it has gotten too complicated for
someone without an engineer's degree and he can't concentrate like he used to, but even so, he is making good money,
thirty-six grand last year, more than Earl with his
schoolteaching in Catamount, more than that bastard Georgie in Rhode Island, working for the state as a fancy-pants
counselor but never writing his own father, never returning
calls. He acts like the old man is dead, for God's sake. What's
wrong with a kid like that, a man in his thirties who won't
speak to his own father? At least Earl deals with him, more
or less, though you'd have thought if one of the boys was
going to hate the father it would be Earl, the elder, who was
so much closer to his mom and was twelve when Nelson left
them and thus probably was her confidant during those
years when she was mad at Nelson for leaving them and not
sending more money. But Georgie, he was always the easy
one, the friendly one. It didn't make sense. Any more than
his dream made sense, the dream in which Nelson strolls into
the room—a kitchen, a bedroom, it's one or the other—and
the woman, Adele or Allie, looks up from her work, ironing,

putting away dishes, unpacking clothes from a trunk, and recognizing him, she points and starts screaming at him, as if to say, "*He's* the one! *He's* the one who killed me, murdered my baby, slew my mother, father, sister, brother! *Him! Him! Him!*"

Despite its insane fury, the dream doesn't weigh on Nelson so much as it angers him. He knows it's about guilt, not redemption, and he's said to himself at least a hundred times that of *course* he feels guilty for the ways he's treated people badly over the years, his wives, his children, others too, old friends who won't talk to him anymore, sisters, brothers-in-law, bosses, even strangers, guys he meets in bars after work and drinks late with and then somehow gets to arguing with, and before he knows how it happens, it has happened again, and there he is, being pulled off some guy and hustled out the door or picked up off the floor and aimed by strangers toward his car. Then he weaves across the lot to his car, gets it started and drives slowly home, where for years Adele and now Allie wait for him, wait to shout at him, or if not to shout, then to glare and snub him and show him their back, until he gets mad all over again and wrecks the careful affection he's built up between them since the last time. Oh, sure, he knows that once every few years he loses control and hits his wife across the face or pushes her away too hard. But he isn't a *wife-beater,* one of those guys who takes out his frustrations on someone who can't defend herself. No, he just loses control once in a while, once in a *great* while, damn it, when he's been hounded, nagged, criticized, picked at, until he just can't stand it anymore, so he lashes back, pushes her away, gets himself left alone, for God's sake, so he can *think.*

Around eight, Nelson takes his third drink. Then, passing from the kitchen through Allie's cluttered office, he goes into the cold, dark barn, where his ten cords of wood are stacked in neat head-high rows along the near wall from the front to the back of the large building. When he returns, chilled, with an armload of wood, he sees his wife at the range, boiling water for tea. Her short blue-gray hair is wet from her shower and slicked back like a boy's, and she's dressed in her usual western clothes, jeans too tight around her big hips and legs and a red-and-white-checked shirt with pearl buttons. Her clothing annoys him, though he never says so directly. "You dress like you want people to think you keep horses," Nelson has told her. With most people (though no longer with him), Allie affects a manliness that Nelson finds disturbing—a hearty, jocular way of speaking. She's a back-slapper, a shoulder-puncher, characteristics that, when he first took up with Allie, attracted Nelson. Long before that, he'd come to despise Adele's whine, her insecurity and depression, so that Allie's good-natured teasing, her tough talk, released him from guilt for a while, maybe a year, maybe two, until he began to see through the bravado to the strangely fragile woman inside, and then, when he hurt her with his hard, unexpected words and once in a while with his hands, too, he began to feel guilty again, just as with Adele. You think a woman's strong, that she can take it, so you treat her as an equal, and before you know it she can't take it, and suddenly you're forced to tiptoe around her as if a single hard step would break her into a thousand weeping pieces. More and more, Nelson believes that being alone is the only clear route to his happiness. It's coming to seem the only way to avoid hurting other people, which in his experience is what gives them power over you. Look at Georgie, his son. The boy has a power over Nelson that derives from his belief that he was hurt by Nelson over twenty years earlier, when the boy was only ten. Earl, now—he's different. Earl's made of tougher stuff. You can't really hurt him; he's like his dad that way. He won't let you close enough to hurt him, and consequently he never obtains any power over you, either. That's the kind of love Nelson both understands and respects. It's what he had with his second wife in the first year or two of their marriage and what he misses in her now.

"You're up, eh," he says to Allie's back, and he dumps the wood into the woodbox, startling the dog awake.

"Yep." The dog gets to her feet and crosses to Allie, shoves her head against the woman's hand until she strokes it between the long, floppy ears. "Ah, you big baby," Allie says. The dog leans her weight against Allie's thigh, and she goes on patting the tall, ungainly animal. It's Allie's dog, not Nelson's—he insists that he doesn't like animals. He's been this way for as long as he can remember. He doesn't know why he is this way, and he doesn't care anymore, if he ever did. It's too late to care. It's how he's survived, and thus it's who he is. Let other people adjust to him—Allie, Earl, Georgie, everyone. If, like Georgie, they aren't willing to adjust, then fine, go away, leave him alone. Alone to think.

"Paper come yet?" Allie asks him.

"You feel like going out to get it, it's there." Nelson has sat back at the table and faces the woodstove, rubbing his hands before it, to get rid of the chill. He's a large, fleshy man and he looks like a bear cleaning its paws after eating.

"You gonna get dressed?" she asks.

"Eventually. It's Sunday."

"I know. I just—"

"What?"

"Nothing." She walks to the refrigerator, pulls a tube of frozen orange juice from the freezer and goes to the sink to prepare it.

"Earl's coming by," he says. "He can bring the paper in from the mailbox."

"Oh? He coming for the wood? It's snowing."

"That's the point. He don't get it now, it'll be there till April." Suddenly, he stands up, and the dog clatters away from the sink, and Allie looks over at him.

"What?" she says.

Nelson is looking intently out the window next to the stove, staring at the driveway and yard, where his son's wood is heaped up.

"What?" she repeats. "Who is it?"

"Leave me alone. For God's sake, leave me alone. I'm trying to think." He moves closer to the window and peers out, as if searching for someone in the snowy distance.

Allie goes back to breaking the frozen orange juice into a green plastic pitcher, and the dog sits on rickety haunches and watches Nelson at the window. "Maybe I should get dressed," he says in a low voice. "So I can help Earl crack that wood loose and load it. Stuff's frozen into the ground, most of it."

Allie says nothing.

"Maybe I'll call him again. See if he's left yet."

"It takes a half hour in good weather. He'll be an hour today," Allie says without looking at him. "You got no hurry." She speaks carefully, slowly, in a deliberately quiet voice.

Nelson dials his son's number, sits down, and lets it ring. On the fourth ring, Earl answers. "Hello?"

"Morning," Nelson says.

"Oh, hi, Dad."

"I was just wondering . . ."

"Yeah, look, I'm sorry. I got sidetracked here, some people came by and we got to talking. Listen, you gonna be there all day today? I can come by later more easily, if that's okay."

"Well, the snow . . ."

"Yeah, I know. You're right. That is good wood. Be nice to get it home here before it gets buried and all."

They are silent for a few seconds, then Earl says to his father, "How about I come out there next Sunday? Or maybe an afternoon this week after school. Yeah, that'd be better all around for me. Though you won't be there then—but we can get together some other time, right?"

"It don't matter much to me one way or the other how you do it—it's your wood, not mine."

"Right."

"All right, then," Nelson says in a voice that's almost a whisper.

"Are you okay, Dad?"

Nelson hesitates a second, ten seconds, twenty. He opens his mouth to speak.

"Dad? You okay?"

"Yeah. I'm . . . I'm fine." His thoughts are burning and whirling, as if there were a terrible conflagration inside his head. "I . . . I wanted to ask you something," he says.

"Sure. About?"

"About . . . I guess about your brother. About Georgie. You. Your mother. Your sister."

"Fine," Earl says. "Shoot."

"No. I mean, not— Well, maybe we oughta talk about this stuff over a few beers or something, you know?"

Earl says, "Hey, fine with me. Anything you say, Dad."

"Well, I was wondering, see, about Georgie. About why he's so mad with me," Nelson blurts, and the fire inside his head roars in his ears, stings his eyes, fills his nostrils and mouth with smoke and ash.

His son says, "Well, you should be asking him that. Not me."

"Yes. Right, of course. You," he says, "you're not mad at me like that, are you? For leaving your mother and all? You know . . . you know what I mean. All that."

Earl inhales deeply, then slowly exhales. "This is weird. This is a weird conversation for us to be having, Dad. I mean, you— Look, I made my peace with all that years ago, and Georgie hasn't, that's all. From his point of view, you ruined his life or something. But that's only how he sees it."

"I didn't, though. I didn't ruin anybody's life. You can't ruin a person's life. I just left, that's all."

"Yeah. It's only a figure of speech."

"I didn't ruin anybody's life."

"Yeah."

"Not your mother's. Not Louise's. Not yours, Earl. Not Georgie's, either."

"No, Dad, not mine. You can be sure of that. Listen, I got to get off, okay? There's people here. I'll be over to dig that wood out sometime this week, some afternoon this week, okay?"

Nelson says fine, that's fine with him, but Earl will have to do it alone, because he is home only on weekends now that winter's here. "I been staying the week down at Seabrook lately," he says.

"No kidding. Where?"

"Oh, I got a room in a motel over in Hampton. It's nice. Color TV. You know. Kitchenette."

"Nice," Earl says.

Nelson says, "I . . . I'm sorry, about that other business, Georgie and all."

"Hey, no sweat, Dad. Look, I gotta go," he says. "Talk to you later, okay?"

"Fine."

"Love to Allie," he says, and then goodbye, and the phone is dead, buzzing in Nelson's hand.

He looks up and sees that his wife is staring at him. He places the receiver on the hook and walks to the sink, pours himself another vodka, only a few ounces, half the glass, and drinks it down with a single swallow. This time he leaves the glass in the sink and the bottle on the drainboard.

"How many's that?" Allie says in a flat, matter-of-fact voice, as if asking him the date. She sips at her tea and over the rim of her cup watches him ignore her. Then she says, "Earl's off in his own world. Don't let him bother you."

"He doesn't bother me. That damn wood bothers me. That's what bothers me."

"Earl doesn't really need it, you know. He lives in town, he just has that little bitty fireplace of his—"

"That's not the *point!*" No, he thinks, the point is that the pile of wood looks like hell out there in the yard, and under the snow it looks somehow worse, because it's no longer clearly firewood but may as well be merely trash or sand or brush or landfill, the dumb, shapeless residue of a job halted when winter came on. Abruptly, Nelson unlatches the gate, passes into the cool, dim living room and walks upstairs to the bedroom. In a short while, he is dressed in heavy green twill pants and wool shirt and snow boots and has returned to the kitchen, where he pulls his mackinaw on, then his black watchcap and thick work gloves.

"You getting the paper?" Allie asks from the table. The dog has settled at her feet.

"Yeah," Nelson grunts. Then quickly he walks out to the barn, where, with the door to Allie's office closed tightly behind him, he shoves open the large sliding door at the front, flooding the darkness with sudden white light and swirls of blowing snow. For a moment he stands, hands sunk in pockets, staring down the driveway to the road, his back to the green rear deck of his Pontiac station wagon and the gloomy darkness of the cavernous barn beyond. He moves around the car to the front door on the driver's side and opens it, reaches under the seat and draws out a half-full pint of vodka. Unscrewing the cap, he tips the bottle up and drinks. It makes no difference—he feels no better or worse for having taken the drink. All he has done is avoid feeling as badly as he would have felt without it. When he has replaced the bottle under the car seat, he turns and bumps against the chopping block, a stump with a steel splitting wedge and single-edged ax driven into its corrugated top. He laughs at himself, and his voice sounds strange to him, an old man's voice—Ho, ho, ho!—mixed with a drunkard's voice—Har, har, har! Hesitating a second at the door, he turns back again, retrieves the bottle from under the car seat, and slides it into his mackinaw pocket. Then he leaves the barn and like an Arctic explorer setting out for the North Pole plunges into the snow.

It's deeper than he expected, eight or ten inches already

and drifting, a heavy, wet snow driven by a hard northeast
wind and sticking to every surface that faces it, trees, houses,
barns, chimneys and now Nelson Painter, working his way
down his driveway from the huge open door of the barn, a
man turning quickly white, so that by the time he reaches
the woodpile he's completely white, even his face, though
he's pulled his head down into his coat as far as he can and
can barely see through the waves of wind-driven snow before him.

He leans over and with one gloved hand grabs at a chunk
of wood, yanks at it, but it won't come. He brushes snow
away, grabs at another, but it, too, won't give. Standing, he
kicks at the first log, and it breaks free of the pile and rolls
over in the snow. He picks it up, lays it against his chest, and
kicks at the second log. He kicks twice, three times, but it
won't come loose, so he takes the first stick, and holding it
by one end, whacks it against the second, until it breaks free.
He's out of breath, sweating inside his coat, cursing the
wood. He picks up the two sticks and goes to work on a third,
which he eventually kicks loose of the pile and picks up and
stacks in his arms, and then, when he kicks at a fourth piece
of wood, he loses his balance, slips, and falls, and the pieces
of wood roll into the snow. Slowly, on his hands and knees
and puffing laboriously now, he gathers up the three logs and
stands, his left hip burning in pain where he fell against it,
and starts back toward the barn.

Halfway there, retracing his nearly filled tracks, he sees
on his left the door to the house pushing slowly open against
the blowing snow, and Allie steps onto the sill and waves an
arm at him, indicating that she wants him to come inside,
to the kitchen. He can't make out her face, but he knows her
look, he's seen it lots of times before, a mixture of anger, hurt
and concern, and he can't hear her because of the wind and
his cap pulled down over his ears, but he knows what she
is shouting to him: "Come inside, for God's sake, Nelson!
You're drunk, and you're going to hurt yourself!" Then the

dog appears beside her, and not recognizing Nelson, bounds outside, barking ferociously at him, leaping eagerly through the snow toward him, barking with great force at the snow-covered stranger in the yard, and when Nelson turns to avoid the animal's rush, he slips on the wet snow and falls again, dropping the wood and scattering it. Suddenly the dog recognizes him and retreats swiftly to the kitchen. Nelson reaches into his coat pocket, pulls out the bottle, works the cap off, and takes a long drink. Recapping the bottle, he places it in his pocket and looks back toward the door, but it's closed. He's alone again. Good. Slowly, he retrieves his three sticks of wood one by one and stands and resumes his trek to the barn. It seems so far away, that dark opening in the white world, miles and years away from him, that he wonders if he will ever get there, if he will spend years, an entire lifetime, out here in the snow slogging his way toward the silent, dark, ice-cold barn where he can set his three pieces of firewood down, lay one piece of wood on the floor snugly against the other, the start of a new row.